"I wonder how our girls would get along." Ross's eyes brightened.

"Hard to say. No one can force a friendship."

He shrugged. "But Peyton could use a friend."

Kelsey's heart ached. "Kids like Lucy and Peyton have a hard time making friends."

"Would you like to give it a try?"

His question sank into her mind. Lucy had made strides making friends over the year of her remission, but Peyton hadn't succeeded. Yet it would mean spending more time with him. She lifted her gaze to his hopeful eyes. "I suppose they might meet...could meet someday."

His face lit up. "Here's an idea. Peyton's birthday is February 14."

"Valentine's Day?" His eager expression wrapped around her heart.

He grinned. "Maybe we could plan something fun."

Her brain and heart faced each other, her brain siding with Lexie's concern while her heart offered hope. An interesting new friend for her, and maybe a new friend for Peyton. A new path for both of them. But a path with no decisive ending, only speculation. Get involved or not?

Books by Gail Gaymer Martin

Love Inspired

*Loving Treasures
*Loving Hearts
Easter Blessings
   "The Butterfly Garden"
The Harvest
   "All Good Gifts"
*Loving Ways
*Loving Care
Adam's Promise
*Loving Promises
*Loving Feelings
*Loving Tenderness
†In His Eyes
†With Christmas in His Heart
†In His Dreams
†Family in His Heart

Dad in Training
Groom in Training
Bride in Training
**A Dad of His Own
**A Family of Their Own

*Loving
†Michigan Islands
**Dreams Come True

Steeple Hill Books

The Christmas Kite
Finding Christmas
That Christmas Feeling
   "Christmas Moon"

GAIL GAYMER MARTIN

A former counselor, Gail Gaymer Martin is an award-winning author of women's fiction, romance and romantic suspense. This is her forty-fifth published novel with over three million books in print. Gail is the author of twenty-seven worship resource books and *Writing the Christian Romance* released by Writer's Digest Books. She is a cofounder of American Christian Fiction Writers, the premier Christian fiction organization in the country.

When not writing, Gail enjoys traveling, presenting workshops at writers' conferences, speaking at churches and libraries, and singing as a soloist, praise leader and choir member at her church, where she also plays handbells and hand chimes. Gail also sings with one of the finest Christian chorales in Michigan, the Detroit Lutheran Singers. Gail is a lifelong resident of Michigan and lives with her husband, Bob, in the Detroit suburbs. To learn more about her, visit her website at www.gailmartin.com. Write to Gail at P.O. Box 760063, Lathrup Village, MI 48076, or at authorgailmartin@aol.com. She enjoys hearing from readers.

A Family of Their Own
Gail Gaymer Martin

Recycling programs
for this product may
not exist in your area.

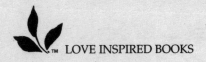

LOVE INSPIRED BOOKS

ISBN-13: 978-0-373-87694-5

A FAMILY OF THEIR OWN

Copyright © 2011 by Gail Gaymer Martin

This is a work of fiction. Names, characters, places and incidents are
either the product of the author's imagination or are used fictitiously, and
any resemblance to actual persons, living or dead, business establishments,
events or locales is entirely coincidental.

This edition published by arrangement with Love Inspired Books.

www.LoveInspiredBooks.com

Printed in U.S.A.

Two are better than one,
because they have a good return for their work:
If one falls down, his friend can help him up.
Also, if two lie down together, they will keep warm.
But how can one keep warm alone?
Though one may be overpowered,
two can defend themselves.
A cord of three strands is not quickly broken.
—*Ecclesiastes* 4:9–10A, 11 & 12

Thanks to Senior Editor Melissa Endlich,
who inspired the idea for this series.
I appreciate her support and the support of
all the staff at Love Inspired who have allowed me
to write stories that touch hearts and lives of
so many people. As always, thanks and love to
my husband, Bob, who understands the crazy life
of a novelist and loves me anyway.

Chapter One

Kelsey Rhodes scanned her friend's living room, her focus drawn to the lovely Christmas tree, its clear miniature lights radiated the same glow in Lexie's eyes. On the mantel a row of white candles flickered in the dusky light. Romantic, for sure. Kelsey's chest expanded, anticipating her friend's wedding ceremony in the cozy setting.

The parents of the bride and groom buzzed with their own excitement, and her chest constricted, seeing Lexie's son, Cooper, dressed in a dark suit, sitting near the window. He looked so cute. When he'd been released from the hospital a few weeks ago, allowing him to be home for Christmas and the January wedding, Kelsey had been relieved for Lexie. Her friend's plight aroused thoughts of her own daughter's illness, in remission for nearly a year. She prayed that Cooper's struggle with leukemia would take the same turn as Lucy's.

The succulent aroma of roast pork drifted into the room. But as delicious the scent was, Kelsey's stomach knotted. The idea of meeting Ross Salburg, Ethan's best man, had set her on edge, and nothing seemed to knock it out of her mind. If he recognized her name or who she was, she would be uncomfortable. Maybe she hadn't tried hard enough to get

Ross into the Mothers of Special Kids organization. She'd tried to explain that the group was only for mothers, but he didn't care. Ethan mentioned that Ross had been disappointed. Facing him for the first time today put a damper on the celebration for her.

The doorbell rang, and Kelsey's pulse soared. She worked a pleasant expression onto her face, knowing the bell offered three options—the groom, the pastor or Ross.

Swallowing her anxiety, she pinned her gaze to the door as Lexie opened it. Nippy air swished into the room along with a man she'd never seen before. His good looks stole her breath. She had no doubt about the stranger's identity, and her stomach churned, facing their introduction.

Lexie steered him around the room, introducing him to the two sets of parents first. Ross leaned over to give Cooper a warm greeting, then faced her. She managed a smile.

"Kelsey, this is our best man, Ross." Lexie grinned. "And this is my matron of honor, Kelsey Rhodes."

Lexie's knowing look set Kelsey on edge. He'd already been told who she was.

Ross extended his hand, an unreadable expression on his face, but Kelsey sat unmoving, captured by his brown eyes, like bittersweet chocolate, that seemed to penetrate her soul. Heat rolled up her chest until she lowered her gaze to his hand. "Nice to meet you, Ross."

"Same here." He gestured toward the empty seat beside her on the sofa. "Do you mind?"

She forced her mind around her response. "Not at all." Her voice sounded pleasant. So far so good. But when he sank onto the cushion, the scent of a mountain woods wrapped around her, losing her in the image.

He looked around the room. "Ethan's late, I assume." He chuckled.

Ross's voice jerked her from the mountain stream to the

glow of the Christmas lights. Her out-of-control feelings confused her, as did Ross's avoidance of the topic she dreaded.

"Are you all hungry? Mom prepared a great dinner." Lexie's voice penetrated Kelsey's fog of preoccupation. "We'll get started once our two key people arrive."

Ross leaned forward. "Are you sure Ethan hasn't left you standing at the altar?"

Lexie grinned. "He'll be here. He loves pork roast."

Everyone chuckled while Kelsey sank deeper into the cushion. At the moment, she felt uneasy, captured beside the best man. Relief would come once the ceremony began.

Ross's arm brushed against hers, and her senses sharpened. She gazed around the room, hoping to cast off her giddy feeling. Using every ounce of concentration, she tuned into the mothers' conversation about life in Florida until she sensed Ross's eyes on her. Her stomach went into a downward spiral.

She turned to him, like a hound picking up the fox's scent. Here it comes, she deduced from the look on his face.

"Are you aware that I'm the Ross you all voted not to include in your support group?"

Kelsey considered telling a lie, but that wasn't her way, nor was it God's way. "I realized who you were when I heard your name." She sounded pathetic, and his pure innocent look made her feel even worse. "I'm sorry it turned out that way."

He didn't speak, though his eyes searched hers.

Feeling defensive, she wanted to explain. "I know I'm the moderator of the support group, but it went to a vote. It's always been a women's organization—you know, Mothers of Special Kids—and I'd hoped you could find another resource out of the ones that I suggested."

Ross touched her arm. "Please. I wasn't trying to embarrass you. I knew it was a long shot." He lowered his eyes.

"Ethan gave me the other support groups' phone numbers, but—"

"We'd never thought of men joining our group." Heat soared to her cheeks. "When we discussed it…" She captured his gaze. "And we did—all the women thought that men didn't really like talking about their feelings."

He flinched.

She wished she'd phrased it differently. "We thought men preferred to get things done, not talk about them."

"But when a man has a seriously ill child, there's little he can do."

The comment twisted in her chest. Lucy's operations for brain tumors tore into her memory. "I understand. I always felt so lonely before MOSK."

With a slight nod, he lowered his head. "It's hard to open up, but I think hearing about others struggling with similar problems would be helpful. I'm sure I would benefit from everyone's experiences."

"Ross, I'm really sorry." She dragged in a breath. "Now that I've heard what you have to say, I could try again in a while."

His gaze drifted to hers. "Thanks." He wove his fingers together and dropped his clenched hands into his lap. "I did call the other agencies, but either the meeting times didn't work for me or some of them had disbanded their groups." He lifted his chin. "I'm Peyton's only parent, and…"

"I understand." Apologizing again offered little solace for the group's rejection. It made sense at the time, but now… She evaded his eyes, and before she could rally, a noise from outside caught everyone's attention.

Cooper's excitement split the air. "It's Ethan."

The doorknob turned, and Ethan stepped into the foyer, snow drifting from his coat as he waved to everyone waiting. He slipped his arm around Lexie and gave her a fleeting kiss. The gesture triggered a flutter of envy in Kelsey. Years had passed since she'd been hugged by a man, let alone been kissed.

Ethan greeted each person, and when he stopped at the sofa, his eyes captured hers. "I see you've met Ross." A grin flickered on his wind-flushed cheeks.

Guilt snaked through her. "Yes, and we've talked."

He gave Ross a wink and shook his hand.

As he headed back to Lexie, the bell rang again. Ethan answered and welcomed their pastor inside, but when he turned toward the archway where Lexie had been standing, Ethan's eyes widened. "Where'd she go?"

His mother laughed. "She's getting ready for her wedding." She shook her finger at him as if he were still her little boy. "You can't see the bride in her finery before the ceremony. You know that."

Ethan's sheepish nod provided Kelsey with motivation to rise. "I'll go check on her." Escaping up the staircase, she reached the top, then slowed and drew in a deep breath. She needed to get her head untangled from Ross's presence. She'd suspected that her concern had focused on Ross's reaction to the MOSK group's veto, but that wasn't it. That would have been easier than the truth. She found him attractive in many ways. Besides his good looks, his vulnerability touched her and opened doors she thought had been closed.

Dealing with her emotions, she knocked on Lexie's bedroom door, and when Lexie told her to enter, Kelsey slipped inside and faltered. "Lexie, you look gorgeous." Kelsey swept to her side and wrapped Lexie in her arms. "Just beautiful." Though she'd seen her friend's wedding dress on the hanger, she hadn't seen it on Lexie. The white A-line satin gown featured a beaded bodice with a rounded neckline and cap sleeves. Lexie's dark wavy hair hung below her shoulders and contrasted with the sparkling crystal beads. Words failed Kelsey.

Lexie's mother wiped tears from her eyes. "I never thought I'd see this day. Never."

The comment jolted Kelsey's recollection. Lexie and her mother hadn't been close in many years, but mending seemed to have occurred. Memories of Kelsey's own lovely wedding came to mind, an amazing day that sadly ended years later when her husband had run off with her best friend. Lexie's marriage, she believed, was made in heaven.

Could she ever dream of such a day? The question winged in her thoughts for a fleeting second to be replaced with Ross's dark eyes. No. If she'd been foolish earlier, that speculation was the topper.

Lexie motioned to the table beneath the window. "Let's not forget the flowers."

Kelsey opened the box and drew out a bouquet of white orchids mingled with stephanotis and ivy. She handed it to Lexie. Corsages of orchids and ivy remained in the box, one for each mother and one for her. She pinned one on Mrs. Carlson, attached her own, then lifted the four boutonnieres from the florist's box. "I'll take these to the men." She looked at Lexie's mother. "Will you bring the other corsage?"

Mrs. Carlson nodded, and Kelsey slipped out the door with the stephanotis and sprigs of ivy, allowing mother and daughter a moment alone.

She descended the stairs and returned to the living room, where she attached the fathers' and Ethan's boutonnieres. When she faced Ross, her fingers trembled as she ran the long pin through his lapel.

"Thanks." He gave her a warm smile.

Mrs. Carlson returned with the corsage for Ethan's mother, and once she'd pinned it on her, she turned to Ethan. "It's time."

Ethan's anxious gaze flew to the staircase as Pastor Tom motioned Ross and Kelsey to join him in front of the fireplace. The candles blurred as tears welled in Kelsey's eyes. She bit the inside of her lip and turned to face the archway.

Lexie floated down the staircase, and Ethan's eyes never left her as he moved toward her. They walked forward hand-in-hand, and the ceremony began.

Kelsey tuned in to the message, but the words took her back to her own marriage fourteen years earlier. The hurt and sadness of the bitter deceit, the loss of a friend and a husband swept over her. When she heard an *amen,* she forced her mind away from her dark thoughts.

Pastor Tom rested his palm on Lexie and Ethan's entwined hands. "By their promises to God and to all of you present, Alexandria and Ethan have bound themselves to one another as husband and wife." He looked from Ethan to Lexie and back, then grinned and shook his head. "What's keeping you? Kiss your bride."

Ethan drew Lexie into his arms, sealing their bond with a kiss, as chuckles and applause dotted the room, but Kelsey didn't laugh. Her chest ached with a longing. The love in Ethan's eyes and the glow in Lexie's attested to the true meaning of marriage, the kind of marriage God wanted for His children. Her own marriage had missed the mark by miles.

Envy flickered through her when Ross's palm touched her arm.

He tilted his head toward the dining room. "Want to?"

Her heart rose to her throat as she tried to decipher his meaning.

He chuckled. "I'm hungry."

She caught on. "You want to help get the meal ready?"

"Definitely."

She moved to his side, and he placed his palm on her back as they strode through the archway. The warmth of his hand rifled down Kelsey's spine. She pressed her lips together and gathered her wits. "Can you carve a pork roast?"

"Sure can. Let me show you what I can do."

Kelsey already knew what he could do to her emotions, and she wasn't ready for that. She hoped he was as deft cutting a roast.

Ross leaned back in his chair, barraged by multiple conversations surging around the dining-room table. But he wasn't really listening. He'd been able to cover his addled thoughts as he and Kelsey worked in the kitchen for a few short minutes before Mrs. Carlson followed them to take over her job as chef for the celebration dinner.

Meeting Kelsey in person tossed his original concept out the window. He'd pictured her as a nose-in-the-air woman who ruled the Mothers of Special Kids with an iron hand, but he'd been very mistaken. He'd witnessed her uneasy apology attempts and realized that she'd tried to be fair by putting it to a vote.

What did bother him was the women's attitude about men. Stereotypical attitude, he could add. Yes, some men couldn't talk about their feelings. Some wanted to take care of things and not deal with emotions. But he'd learned that emotions were real whether he wanted to feel them or not, and when it came to his daughter, the pain of her struggle wrenched his heart. Why would mothers assume that fathers didn't hurt and didn't wrestle with decisions?

But today wasn't the day to deal with that issue. Maybe no day was right. He had questions for Kelsey, but they were more personal. How was her daughter's health now? Ethan had told him once that her daughter had a brain tumor, but what kind of tumor? Where was Kelsey's husband? Gone, yes. She'd mentioned being alone, but had he died or walked out on her? Had the tension of their daughter's illness caused the rift?

He sounded like a detective, and it unsettled him. Instead of brooding, Ross forced his mind to focus on the ensuing conversation about the upcoming Super Bowl. As he listened and tossed in a comment here and there, Kelsey's presence invaded his space. Her sweet fragrance filtered past before being covered by the yeasty dinner rolls and succulent pork roast.

"Excuse me, please."

Kelsey's voice swept past him, and he gazed at her.

"I need to check on Lucy." She pushed back her chair.

Concerned, Ross shifted and rose. "Is she okay?" He drew her chair aside so she could rise.

Kelsey stood, her body close to his. "She's fine. My sitter isn't the usual one I hire, so I'm always cautious." She slipped past him, and he watched her slide a door aside behind them and enter a room.

He stood a moment, wondering if he should stand until she returned or settle back in his chair again. The time stretched, and his concern rose. Not comfortable nosing into her business, yet not at ease ignoring her absence, he strode toward the door, but as he approached, it slid open and Kelsey stepped out. A questioning look spread across her face.

His mind slowed down, and he could only mumble. "I wanted to make sure you were okay."

A grin replaced her uncertainty. "You're as bad as I am."

He shrugged. "Not bad really. Alert."

"So you're a worrier, too." She tilted her head toward the kitchen. "Should we help clear the dishes?"

"That's a plan." He followed her around the table, removing the soiled china and silverware. Though Mrs. Carlson offered to help, Kelsey suggested that she enjoy the company while they took care of the dishes.

Ross rinsed while Kelsey loaded the dishwasher, and as they worked, he caught her eyeing him on occasion as if she were weighing her feelings about him. When he was about to be blunt and ask, she closed the dishwasher door and rested her hip against the countertop. "Are you always this nice?"

The question caught him off guard. "You mean am I always helpful?"

"Nice. Helpful. I suppose they go hand in hand."

He grinned, still wondering what had brought on that question. "I try to be. How about you?"

Her eyes widened as if surprised at his directness. "I try to calm storms, but sometimes I create new waves. I think being a peacemaker is a good attribute, but I don't know other people's take on me."

He'd expected a playful response. Instead he'd gotten a truthful answer. Earlier when they talked, he'd witnessed her penchant for making peace when she'd offered to bring his name up before the MOSK organization again. "I suppose we never know what people think." He turned off the tap water and rested against the countertop beside her. "I'd like to hear about Lucy." Seeing her expression, he'd surprised her again.

"We've been very blessed. Lucy's been in remission now for nearly a year, and I'm hopeful the last surgery was the end."

"Last surgery?"

"Yes, over the past few years, she had multiple surgeries for brain tumors and—"

"Multiple tumors? I didn't know." His chest tightened. "Are they—"

"Benign."

The constriction in his chest eased, and he inhaled. "That's a relief."

She nodded, but no joy brightened her face. "The problem is the damage each surgery can cause. I fear that a tumor will infiltrate a major part of the brain that will make…" She closed her eyes.

Ross drew closer and rested his hand on her arm. "You've gone through a lot, Kelsey. Any type of tumor is awful."

When she opened her eyes, his tenderness greeted her.

"Thanks. We're so blessed to have things go this way. I wish it could happen to every sick child."

So did he.

He hadn't meant for the conversation to take a dark turn. "You know Ethan's involved with the Dreams Come True Foundation," he noted.

Her eyes met his. "Yes." She chuckled. "That's where Lexie met Ethan. He did a presentation at our MOSK meeting."

"I suppose I'd heard that." Naturally she knew. He shrugged. "Since Lucy is doing so well, have you ever thought of letting her have a dream come true?"

Her smile faded and she flicked a shoulder. "I suppose I'm silly, but it seems like tempting fate."

"Tempting fate?"

"Like taking her health for granted. I've always felt having her well is dream enough."

He didn't know how to respond. She seemed too positive to step into such a dark thought. Silence smothered conversation.

"Ross."

His heart kicked.

"Tell me about Peyton." Interest brightened the mood.

Peyton. Even her name grabbed at his emotions. She'd been through so much. Kelsey would understand, but he wrestled with the ability to speak.

This time Kelsey touched his arm. "Another time, Ross. I didn't mean to hit you with that question today."

The reprieve relieved him. Talking about Peyton homed in on so many things that hurt. A wedding celebration didn't seem like an appropriate place to open up those wounds. But she'd suggested another time, and the idea gave him hope. "I'd like that."

A frown settled on her face. "You'd like what?"

"To talk another time." Making a date with a woman arose like a vague memory. "Maybe dinner sometime?"

An unreadable expression flashed across her face.

"With the girls, if you like." He caught his error. "But then it would be too difficult to talk."

Her features softened and a smile lit her eyes. "Dinner would be nice."

As he was about to set a date, Lexie's mother darted into the kitchen. He closed his mouth. Before the evening ended, Ross needed to ask for her telephone number, and he hoped by then that she hadn't rethought his invitation and decided it wasn't a good idea.

Kelsey stood in Lexie's kitchen rinsing off the last dishes, her mind on Ross. Lexie had taken her mother upstairs to tell her what she needed to know about Cooper's medicine. Mr. and Mrs. Carlson had offered to stay with Cooper for a week while Lexie and Ethan enjoyed a honeymoon cruise. Knowing Lexie's past with her mother, Kelsey marveled at the reestablished relationship. God had shined on them during their time together.

The countertops were cleared and the food stashed away. Kelsey poured another cup of coffee, hoping it was decaf, and she sank onto the breakfast nook bench, not wanting to leave before saying goodbye to Lexie. Ross had suggested dinner, and she'd readily agreed. When he'd asked for her telephone number, she had given him her cell phone number, but then had second thoughts. She'd only met the man today and, the more she thought about it, accepting a dinner date seemed a little premature. Maybe a coffee date would have been better.

Still, Ross intrigued her. She'd never known a man so open about his emotions. His love for his daughter shone on his face, and yet she saw something else, an expression that aroused her attention. Ross had a story to tell, and she wanted to hear it. His behavior infiltrated her mind. So often she resisted talking about her problems, but with him it had been easy to be open.

"Kelsey."

She jumped upon hearing her name and hurried to the head of the stairs. "I'm here."

"Come up."

As she ascended the staircase, Mrs. Carlson came down. A pleasant look filled her face, and it triggered an unexpected joy in Kelsey's heart. Forgiveness. Understanding. Whatever had happened between Lexie and her mother resulted in happiness for Lexie. At the top of the stairs, she faltered. "Where are you?"

"In here."

The voice came from her bedroom, and Kelsey strode to the doorway and stopped. "Need help?"

Lexie turned to face her. "No. You've given me all the help I need." She opened her arms and Kelsey walked into her embrace. "Thanks so much for being my matron of honor and for all your support. You've become a great friend."

"You, too." The words caught in her throat, thinking of all the dark times they'd shared with their children's illnesses. "I can't tell you how happy I am for you."

"Ethan's one in a million." Lexie motioned for her to sit.

"He is." She shifted to the only chair in the room and sank into the cushion. "But I'm not just referring to Ethan. I'm also talking about your mother."

"It's been amazing, hasn't it?" Tears glinted in her eyes. "I never expected Mom to come around as she's done, and it shows how good forgiveness can be."

The comment pierced Kelsey. She could only nod. Forgiveness was something she'd never granted to her ex-husband and to her friend who'd betrayed her.

After shifting her suitcase to the side, Lexie sat on the edge of the bed and gazed at her. The look sent an uneasy feeling through Kelsey. She waited, trying to understand what had happened to their conversation. No doubt Lexie had something to say, and Kelsey couldn't guess what it might be. The waiting made her raw. "What's wrong?"

Lexie shook her head and lowered her eyes. "This is really none of my business."

Kelsey froze. Business? "Did I do something wrong? If I did—"

"No. No. It's only…" She drew in a lengthy breath. "I'm surprised that you and Ross hit it off so well."

"Why?" She studied Lexie's face. "He handled the MOSK rejection pretty well."

She shrugged. "He seemed to."

"Then what?"

"When you and Ross were flirting, I thought it was cute… at first, but—"

"Flirting?" She bristled that her response to Ross had been so obvious.

Lexie shook her head again. "Why don't I shut up? It's your life."

"My life?" Her mind raced. Maybe Ross was married, and she didn't realize it or maybe… Her confusion split the air. "Explain what you're talking about. You can't stop now."

"I'm being silly." Lexie closed her eyes and tilted her head back, filling her lungs. "I sound like a soap opera." She lowered her chin. "It's only that you and Ross both have kids who need so much. Yes, Lucy is doing well now, and we both hope that it's forever, but from what I know Peyton has a long road ahead of her, and I wonder if you and Ross are wise to get involved. It seemed so obvious to me that—"

"Get involved? Lexie, we only met today. Yes, we were bonded by his name coming up at the MOSK meeting and he happened to be your best man. He's very nice, and we have something in common, but we aren't planning…" We're having dinner. That fact raced through her mind, along with how interesting she found him. "We aren't planning a life together."

Lexie rose and approached her as she opened her arms. "But I've never seen you so animated with anyone. You're a down-to-business person, and you're a peacemaker. I've seen many sides of you, but I'd never seen you so alive. Maybe you didn't sense what I did, but you and Ross...I don't know. Maybe I'm delusional."

Kelsey sat in the chair, staring at her open arms, an obvious invitation for a hug, but at the moment, she didn't want to be hugged. Her chest ached and her head spun. What in the world had happened to stir Lexie's imagination? It made no sense. Yes, she acknowledged her interest in Ross. Despite second-guessing herself, she'd enjoyed the conversation once she got over the uncomfortable introduction. Why would anyone, especially Lexie, see anything wrong with her friendship with Ross?

Lexie's arms remained open, expectation on her face.

Forcing herself from the chair, Lexie stepped into her arms. "I will never do anything to hurt Lucy. Don't ever worry about that. My happiness today was for you, dear friend." She drew back and took her hands. "Now, go on your honeymoon and have a wonderful time. I'm a big girl, and I'll use wisdom before jumping into anything."

A faint smile crept onto Lexie's face. "I shouldn't have said anything. I'm being silly."

Kelsey agreed, but she let it drop. She always used good judgment when it came to Lucy and sound thinking for her own life.

But today she felt different, almost as if her life had been on hold until now.

Chapter Two

Ross sat in the hospital waiting room while Peyton had a heart echo and an MRI. The clock hands inched around the face while his mind moved at the same pace. He stared at his cell phone, Kelsey's phone number in his hand. He'd been adventurous enough to ask her to dinner, but today his enthusiasm faded. Her blunt responses and quick honesty challenged him to respond as she did—in an open and direct manner. He couldn't.

On the other hand, he enjoyed her company and personal enjoyment was something he'd hooked to an anchor and dropped into Lake St. Clair. Boats disappeared in that lake, and their occupants were never located. He thought his anchor would never be found, but it rose to the surface five days ago when he laid eyes on Kelsey.

He glanced at the clock again. Peyton's tests never took this long. The heel of his shoe tapped against the shining marble floor of the heart unit. He pressed his dry lips together and refocused on the cell phone. He needed a distraction. And good news. Checking the numbers she'd scribbled on the notepaper, he punched them in and waited.

Three rings. Four. Leave a message or not? His question vanished when he heard the connection. "Kelsey, this is Ross."

"Ross."

He waited, the sound of her surprise ringing in his ears. "I called to set a date for dinner." Maybe he should have suggested coffee. "Whatever time is best for you."

Silence. Ross could almost feel the electrical current zinging in her brain.

"I—I'm not sure this is a good time to make plans."

The muscles in his jaw tightened. "Is Lucy ill?"

"No. But things are hectic here."

Hectic? He could read her thoughts as he listened to silence.

Kelsey cleared her throat. "Lucy's decided to get more involved at school, and between my job, running her places and keeping an eye on her health, I—"

"You're tired." He knew the routine, and he didn't want to hear her excuses. She'd done what he suspected and had second thoughts. "I've been sitting at the hospital for nearly two hours waiting while Peyton has some tests."

"I hate waiting. Time drags horribly." The tension in her tone had eased.

Ross shifted in the chair. "Magazines aren't great company."

"So true."

Silence.

"Ross, I'm sorry we didn't finish our conversation about Peyton. I don't even know what kind of illness she has."

The word stuck in his throat. He sucked in air. "Cardiomyopathy."

A gasp echoed into the receiver. "I'm so very sorry. How bad is she?"

"I try to be hopeful." He'd been optimistic during his wife's illness, too. Ruthie had been so sure she would live to be a mother to her daughter. "These tests will let me know how she's progressing."

"More waiting."

The line hummed with silence, and he lifted his shoulders, knowing he needed to say goodbye.

"Let me know what the doctors say, okay?" Her voice breezed from the line, a different spirit than he'd heard earlier.

"Sure." He'd have Ethan tell her. "I need to—"

"Ross."

His flesh prickled. "Yes."

"About dinner. I can get a sitter for Friday, I think, if that works for you."

He stopped breathing. "Friday?" Confusion skittered along his frame, but he gathered his wits. "Works for me. How about if I pick you up at six?"

"Six is good." She gave him her address.

His gaze drifted to the clock. "I'll see you then."

She said goodbye, and he tucked his cell phone into his pocket as he rose. The wait addled him, but not as much as it did Kelsey. He lifted his shoulders and eyed the volunteer at the desk. Maybe she'd have some information on Peyton's status. As he strode toward her, a nurse called his name from the doorway. When he turned, she beckoned him to follow.

Though relief washed over him, he also succumbed to dread. He followed the young woman, knowing he could hear good news or bad from the doctor, or maybe today nothing at all. Life seemed like one long delay.

The nurse paused outside a consultation room. "You can wait in here with Peyton. The doctor will see you soon."

He thanked her and stepped inside.

Peyton sat in a chair, looking so young despite her constant reminders. "I'm almost twelve, Dad. I'm not a baby anymore."

To him, she'd always be his baby. But he knew better than to say that to her. "How did it go?"

"Same thing every time. Don't move. Hold my breath." She shrugged. "You know the drill."

He nodded and sat in the only other chair in the room. "But you've been doing well, right?"

She shrugged again. "I guess."

Attitude grew with age. He realized that. His daughter was on the cusp of her teens and nearly a woman in so many ways.

"Mr. Salburg."

He looked up as Dr. Timmons stepped through the doorway. The doctor closed the door and leaned against it. "We'll need to read the results more thoroughly, but for now, things look pretty much status quo."

Ross's pulse skipped. Status quo was better than a decline in her health, but he so longed to hear the word *improvement.* "That means no real changes."

"My main concern is Peyton's recurring arrhythmia. She is taking her blood thinner as directed, right?"

Ross nodded.

"Once we read the tests, we'll know if we have to up her blood thinner. I hate to do it because that will restrict her physical activities a little more."

Peyton groaned. "I don't want restrictions."

His gaze shifted to her. "I know you don't like that, but it's for your safety. Blood thinners prevent blood clots, and that can happen when the heart gets out of rhythm. We've talked about this before."

They had, and while Peyton would say nothing more in front of the physician, Ross would hear her complaints on the way home. Physical restriction upset her, because she felt different than the other kids. Peyton wanted to be normal, like everyone else. She wasn't.

Dr. Timmons pulled his back from the door. "But the good

news is, from what I see, your heart looks about the same. No new dilation, and that's great."

"So what's next?" Ross rose from the chair, his focus on Peyton.

"When I receive the full report, I'll give you a call. For now, follow the same medication protocol." He stepped aside and pulled open the door. "I'll see you again, Peyton."

She gave a nod, and when Dr. Timmons's back was turned, she rolled her eyes.

"I know, honey, but the medication is keeping you safe."

"Right." Another eye roll.

Frustration coiled through Ross. He longed to have the right words to offer her hope, but she had to grasp that herself. When it came from him, he received eye rolls and nasty looks. He'd do anything to take away her illness. His thoughts diverged from the stress. It's the only way he could deal with it all. The phone call came to mind and then Kelsey's plight. How did she handle the situation with her daughter?

Kelsey gazed at the barnlike structure of Peabody's Restaurant, one of her favorites. Ross had suggested a few places for dinner, and she appreciated his thoughtfulness. Besides delicious food, the restaurant had reasonable prices.

Ross walked beside her and pulled open one of the double doors at the entrance. They climbed the few stairs and turned into the dining area. Once seated in a cozy nook on the second floor, Kelsey focused on the man who'd tried to be so kind—the first man who'd tugged at her heart since her husband. Her stomach knotted as she tried to cope with the new emotion.

"Kelsey, I hope your accepting this invitation isn't because you feel sorry for me. That's something I don't want from any—"

"Ross, no. Not at all." As she pled innocence, her mind shot back to the call and what had triggered her acceptance.

His loneliness. The waiting. Was that pity? She struggled for an explanation. "Yes, it had to do with the long wait and wondering, but it's not pity. It's different. It's mutual understanding. I need someone to talk with about those things, and I have the mother's group. MOSK has been a relief for me. It's a place where I don't burden others with my woes because they understand." She looked into his questioning eyes. "I relate to your situation. I've been there."

He looked down at the table and then up again. "I guess that's why I was disappointed when your group said no. The time and place are so convenient for me. It fits my schedule, but maybe you're right. Maybe a man sitting with all those women would put a damper on their openness. I don't want to do that."

Her chest ached for him while her mind flipped to a new awareness. "I don't think we thought of you as an individual, Ross."

Confusion filled his face.

"We thought of you as a gender. Man or woman—some of us need support, and we weren't thinking along those lines. I'll pursue this topic with them. You need people dealing with the same problem you're struggling with. A child with a serious illness. Our vote seems selfish, now that I think about it."

"Not selfish. I think you were being protective."

He'd hit it on the head.

Ross reached across the table and touched her hand. "I only want you to do what's best for the group. I'll survive. I always have."

And so had she. Alone. Miserable at times. Afraid. Hopeful. That had become her life. She nodded. "So tell me about Peyton. You said she has cardiomyopathy."

"Dilated cardiomyopathy."

"I didn't know there were different types."

He shook his head. "It's the most common. The heart enlarges and stretches because it's weak and can't pump normally to move blood through the chambers. The problem can lead to arrhythmia and issues with the heart's electrical system."

And death. The thought chilled her. Kelsey studied his face as he talked about Peyton's treatments and medication. How did he cope with it all and with such patience? She'd gone through many things with Lucy's brain tumors but, praise God, they were benign and since the last surgery, they'd seemed to lick it. "It's too much for a child. How old is she?"

"Peyton will celebrate her twelfth birthday next month."

"Lucy's almost eleven. That's sure something we have in common."

She grinned. "You mean the 'attitude.'"

"You got it."

They both grew silent. Ross's hand rested near hers, and she longed to reach out and hold it against her heart. The man had gone through too much without a partner, and though she wanted to know about that, too, she held back. One step at a time.

Yet Lexie's concern still rang in her ears. *I wonder if you and Ross are wise to get involved.* A friendship wasn't really getting involved. Yes, she found Ross attractive, and attraction could grow. But she didn't have time for involvement. For romance. The whole idea threw her off balance. She needed to stick to her friends.

"Are you ready to order?"

Kelsey's head jerked up and gazed at the waitress. "Sorry. I haven't even looked at the menu."

"Could we have a few more minutes?" Ross winked at the young woman.

"Certainly. Take your time, unless you'd like to order drinks now."

They placed their drink orders, and when the waitress left, they pored over the menu. But Kelsey's concentration drifted to their girls. Both struggled to fit into a normal world, and that wasn't always possible. If the girls met, it might be good for them. Lucy connected with Cooper because he had a serious illness. Scenarios rolled through her mind, envisioning Lucy and Peyton together. Obviously, a friendship with Ross without the girls' involvement would be impossible. Their daughters took priority in their lives. Maybe the friendship could be a good thing.

"Penny for your thoughts."

Ross's voice startled her.

"Or should I offer five bucks. You look mighty serious."

"Sorry, I was thinking of our girls." Honesty without details. She hated her urge to hide her thoughts. Conjecture didn't make sense at this point. "Have you heard anything about her recent tests?"

He drew in a lengthy breath. "Probably next week."

"Please let me know how it goes." She almost wished she hadn't asked, but she cared. Not even knowing the child, she cared.

"I will. And thanks for being concerned."

"Hopeful is more like it."

He rested his hand on hers. "I like your attitude."

The word *attitude* gave them a chuckle. Lucy had developed one recently that Kelsey wanted to nip in the bud, as her mother used to say.

Ross looked thoughtful. "I wonder how our girls would get along." His eyes brightened.

"Hard to say. No one can force a friendship."

He shrugged. "But Peyton could use a friend."

Her heart ached. "Kids like Lucy and Peyton have a hard time making friends."

"Would you like to give it a try?"

His question sank into her mind. Lucy had made strides making friends over the year of her remission, but Peyton hadn't succeeded. Yet it would mean spending more time with Ross. She lifted her gaze to his hopeful eyes. "I suppose they might meet…could meet someday."

His face lit up. "Here's an idea. Peyton's birthday is February 14."

"Valentine's Day?" His eager expression wrapped around her heart.

He grinned. "Maybe we could plan something fun."

"Are you sure Peyton would like that?"

His grin faded. "I would hope so."

"Well, I'd have to check with Lucy." Her brain and heart faced each other, her brain siding with Lexie's concern while her heart offered hope. An interesting new friend for her, and maybe a new friend for Peyton. A new path for both of them. But a path with no decisive ending, only speculation. Get involved or not?

A Robert Frost poem slipped into her mind, one of her favorites, "The Road Not Taken." Two paths. One decision. And, as the poem said, which path she chose would make all the difference.

Ross sat in his recliner, watching the six o'clock news, while his mind skipped above the latest world disasters to his dinner with Kelsey. She ran hot and cold. It confused him. Their conversations were good—meaty sometimes—and other times, they were both chuckling at commonalities between the girls or situations in their lives. But the next minute, she drifted off to another planet. One that seemed so distant and dark.

He'd sensed that she liked him. At least enjoyed his company, but her hesitation drove him crazy. Point blank, he needed to ask her what was up. Yet as soon as the thought hit his mind, the possibility of her honest answer discouraged him. Maybe it wasn't what he wanted to hear.

He clenched his teeth. Why look for problems? She'd more

or less agreed to celebrate Peyton's birthday and bring Lucy along. He could only pray that the girls liked each other.

Peyton's negativity had gotten under his skin. Still, the poor kid had gone through so much that he avoided nagging her about it. She'd been brave for the past years dealing with that horrible illness. God had spared her thus far. Much longer than her mom had survived once diagnosed with the disease. That gave him prayerful hope.

"Peyton." He leaned forward and looked toward the doorway.

No response.

"Peyton?" But this time he flipped the footrest down and rose. No sense in calling like a truck driver. He wandered across the room and through the archway to her bedroom door. "Peyton, are you in there?" He heard a thump followed by her footsteps.

She pulled open the door. "What?"

Ross pursed his lips, holding back a comment that circled in his mind. "Can we talk a few minutes?" He looked past her into the wonderful sitting area that had once been his. He'd made a true sacrifice giving her the master-bedroom suite, but other than the small guestroom where he slept, the other bedrooms were upstairs. His shoulders dropped as he drew his attention back to Peyton. "Your birthday is coming up, and I thought we should talk about it."

"Dad, I don't want a party. I'm—"

"No party. I understand." She'd missed so much school over the last years that friendships weren't easy for her. The kids treated her like someone too delicate to befriend. It hurt him to see her in that situation.

"Then what?" She raised her round hazel eyes, so like her mother's.

"Can I come into your room?" He motioned toward the two chairs in the sitting area, matching recliners Ruthie had picked out for them.

She stepped into the hallway and closed the door.

He stood back and followed her into the family room. She sank onto the couch as he settled back into his recliner. If he could figure out Peyton's moods, it would certainly help. "What would you like to do?"

"I'd like to read my book." She motioned toward her bedroom.

He bit back his frustration. "I mean for your birthday." He'd given it thought but telling her what he had in mind would put an end to that.

"Could we just go out to dinner?"

Dinner. He could do that. "Mexican? I know you like Azteca."

Her nose curled. "Japanese."

He grinned. "Benihana's?" She loved the chefs entertaining the guests with their cooking prowess. But Kelsey and Lucy? He hoped they like Japanese food. "Benihana's is fine." The muscles in his stomach contracted. "I have another idea, too. It'll make it more like a party."

A scowl settled on her face as she tilted her head. "I told you I don't want a party."

"Not a real party, but a celebration."

Her eyes probed his.

"I know a lady who has a daughter your age. She's been sick, too, and I thought maybe we could invite them. Her mother thought it would be nice."

Her scowl deepened. "Can't it just be us?"

The conversation with Kelsey marched through his mind. "I sort of invited them already. I thought you'd be happy." That wasn't exactly the truth. "I hoped you'd be happy."

"Dad." She bolted up from the sofa. "Do whatever." She marched through the archway.

So much for beginning the birthday celebration on a high note. Now what? Should he call Kelsey and cancel? Kelsey's face filled his mind, her sapphire-blue eyes, her blond hair combed back with its stubborn part. He pictured her running her long fingers through the strands as if the action would ban the part from appearing. It never did.

He loved her smile—though rarer than her serious look—her full lips curved at the ends and smile lines like parentheses, as if the smile were an afterthought. If he called and canceled, that could end everything.

Chapter Three

❧

"Touchdown!"

Kelsey jumped at Bill Rueben's outburst. Noise reached its pitch as the touchdown tied the score. Kelsey didn't care if anyone won, but she wouldn't admit that to a soul. Two things had motivated her to come to Lexie and Ethan's Super Bowl party. First, Lexie had invited her to see her honeymoon photos. Seven days on a Caribbean cruise sounded wonderful, especially living in Michigan with only graying snow piled along the curbs outside the window. But most of all, she knew that Ross had been invited.

"Grab food when you want it." Lexie stood in the archway to the living room. "Chips and dip, salsa and sub sandwiches." She stepped back and then peeked around the corner. "And cookies. Homemade."

Kelsey wriggled free from her seat on the sofa and rose. She ambled to the doorway and stood a moment, taking a furtive peek at Ross in a chair near the window. He'd said hello and asked about Lucy. She'd asked about Peyton, but with so many people watching them, she hadn't prolonged the conversation. In the light through the window, his dark hair shone with glints of mahogany. He wore it thick, with a slight widow's peak that most women would envy. He had a great smile, but he wasn't Adonis. His sensitivity captured her more. And she liked his appealing ways.

Today he'd worn jeans and a teal-colored sweater. His shoulders looked as wide as an ocean—maybe a Great Lake. She snickered to herself. Whenever Ross came to mind, a giddy feeling rustled through her. When she was near him, her pulse raced.

She studied him for a moment, and before turning away, he glanced up and saw her gazing at him. She flinched when he grinned. She managed a pleasant expression before she strutted into the dining room, forcing her attention on the food spread across the table. But a noise in the kitchen drew her toward Lexie, who stood behind the island, preparing coffee. Kelsey sank a chip into the dip, popped it in her mouth and headed her way. "Where are your honeymoon photos?"

"On the computer in the den." She motioned toward the sliding door off the dining room. "There's an icon on the desktop. Click on it, and it will take you right to the photos. I put captions under the pictures so in a couple years I'll remember where I was." Though she behaved lighthearted, her expression said she had something on her mind.

Kelsey strode deeper into the kitchen, drawn by curiosity as much as the scent of the brewing coffee. "Cooper's with Ethan's mom?"

She nodded. "You want to grab some food?" She motioned to the breakfast nook and headed that way, a cookie in her hand.

Food didn't arouse Kelsey's interest at that moment, nor did the coffee. She followed Lexie and slipped onto the bench across from her. They sat, eyeing each other as if words had taken a vacation. Kelsey's mind skipped around possibilities of what Lexie wanted. It couldn't be marital problems, but what about Cooper's health? "You have something on your mind."

She looked down. "You know, I was really weird with you

a few weeks ago. About Ross and you. I don't know what got into me."

"Forget it. On your wedding day, you're allowed to do and say whatever you like. All is forgiven."

"But it's not like me to butt into someone's life. I told Ethan what I'd done, and he wasn't happy. He told me Ross is a great guy, and he deserved a little pleasure in life, just as you do."

A knot formed in Kelsey's throat. She cleared it. "Hey, it's no big deal."

Lexie grasped her hand. "Everyone needs friends, and for some reason, my mind jumped to romance. I suppose I could blame that on my wedding day." She gave a feeble chuckle.

"Wedding days can arouse all kinds of emotions. Think of the brides who run away and the grooms who don't show up." She squeezed Lexie's hand. "Really. Forget it."

Lexie lowered her head, then lifted it again with a grin. "Have you two seen each other?"

Kelsey gave a toss of her head. "He's in the living room." She liked the sneaky way she avoided the question.

"You know what I mean. A date? A…coffee or lunch? Maybe a movie and dinner?" Lexie searched her face and arched an eyebrow. "Nothing?"

This question she couldn't sidestep. "We went to dinner. At Peabody's. We talked about the kids and he took me home."

"And that's it?" She drew back, a look of disbelief on her face. "I haven't brought him up to you on the phone because I wanted to apologize in person, and you didn't say anything to me." She shook her head again. "I thought there would be more. You both seemed so taken with each other that day."

Air bottled in Kelsey's lungs. She released it. "He mentioned getting the girls together for Peyton's birthday. It's coming up."

"So this is where you're hiding."

Kelsey jumped as Ross's voice sailed past. He stood at the

island, a sub sandwich resting on a paper plate in his hand. She searched his face, wondering if he'd heard their conversation.

"Girl talk." Lexie gave her a pat and rose. "Help yourself to some coffee. I just made it."

His gaze slipped to Kelsey. "Did I interrupt something?"

Ignoring his question, Kelsey scooted from the bench. "I came in to ask Lexie about looking at the honeymoon photos." She strutted to the island and leaned forward, trying to see through the dining-room archway. "The game's not over, is it?"

He grinned. "It's just about halftime." He set his plate on the island counter and wandered over to the coffeepot. "Cups?"

Lexie pulled a few mugs from an overhead cabinet. "Milk? Sugar?"

"Black?" He turned to Kelsey. "Coffee?"

She nodded and ambled his way. "Thanks."

"Can guys see the photos, too?" He looked over his shoulder and gave a wink.

Lexie chuckled. "They're in the den. Kelsey knows where they are."

Kelsey's pulse tripped.

"Do you mind?" He faced her and offered her the coffee mug he'd filled for her.

"Not at all." She took the mug, the aroma drifting around her, though she could still catch the scent of Ross's aftershave.

She led the way but stopped when he paused to pile a few chips on his plate before following her. When he came into the room, he slid the door closed behind him. He grinned and slipped past her.

She swiveled in the desk chair and watched him set his mug and plate on the lamp table before he sank into the love seat. "Are you ready for the photos?"

He put the end of the sub into his mouth and took a bite. "I can eat and do anything." He grinned again and dug a paper napkin from his pocket to wipe his mouth. "My mother taught me not to talk with my mouth full."

She couldn't hold back a chuckle. "I think your mother failed." She motioned to the monitor. "Can you see?"

He set the sandwich back onto the plate. "If you turn the monitor a little, I can see fine."

She tilted the screen and rolled her chair back as she hit the button for the slide show. The photographs began—luscious blue skies, golden sand, palm trees and sugarcane plants. So many lovely photos slid past while she longed to be somewhere beneath that glinting sunshine, but not alone. Her mind replaced the faces in the photos. All the pictures of Lexie and Ethan grinning at the camera at dinner, walking the beach, sitting in an aerial tram surrounded by jungle became Ross and her. Kelsey released a shuddered breath and jerked her wayward thoughts back. "What I wouldn't give for a trip like that."

Ross rose and moved beside her, closer to the monitor. "It does make me envious." He motioned to the lovely landscape photo. "Look at that sunlight. Now look out the window." He crouched beside her, resting his hand on the chair arm and leaning closer to the photos.

Though she knew the view out the window, her gaze was drawn to the snow-covered shrubs and tree limbs in Lexie's backyard. When she looked back, their eyes met. Blood pounded through her veins, a ridiculous reaction to looking at photos. She struggled to pull her gaze away and sought a new topic. "Are Lexie and Ethan going to stay in this house? I thought Ethan had a nice place, too."

"He does, but I heard they're thinking of Cooper. He loves it here, and for now, I think they're staying with what's familiar for him."

"That's really considerate." And no surprise. That's the kind of man Ethan was.

Ross looked thoughtful. "I'd do that, too, I think."

Her stomach tightened. They both would, so where did that leave them? "We give a lot when our kids are sick." She clicked off the photographs and leaned back in the chair.

He gazed at her. "And it's not always easy, is it?" He pushed himself up, hands against his thighs and stretched. "Before we join the others, I wanted to check with you about Peyton's birthday." He resettled on the love seat. "Did you talk with Lucy?"

Something about his expression didn't sit well with her. "She's fine with it." She guessed.

Ross's problem. "What about Peyton? What does she want? It's her birthday."

He lowered his head and leaned forward, elbows on his knees, hands folded. "I did have to deal with a little attitude."

The change of plans she'd anticipated. A blend of relief and disappointment swirled through her.

He raised his head, a slight grin on his lips. "But she ended the conversation by leaving it up to me."

A similar situation with Lucy plodded into her mind. She rose. "I think we should drop it. It's Peyton's birthday, and it should be her decision."

A frown conquered his faint grin. "No, please. Let me explain." He patted the seat beside him.

Kelsey eyed the empty cushion, weighing her emotions. She felt safer in the chair, but he looked forlorn. The moment called for listening. She rolled the chair back to the desk, and sat beside him.

"Here's the thing." Ross caught her gaze. "Peyton often feels rejected by other kids. She's missed a lot of school, and she doesn't feel like part of her class most of the time. The kids aren't mean or anything, but you know kids. The boys are boys at that age, and the girls have their little cliques. Peyton doesn't seem to fit into any of them."

Her heart squeezed, remembering. "Lucy missed school, too, but she's doing okay. It takes time, Ross. Encourage Peyton to be patient."

"I tell her that, but she's not willing to wait. She wants things when she wants them, and when they don't happen, she rejects them. I'm afraid that's what she's done with the kids at school. I asked her teacher, and she said Peyton is rather standoffish."

Kelsey pressed her lips together to hold back her comment. Her life revolved around helping people solve problems, and sometimes keeping her mouth closed was the best choice.

"I think that having a friend would help her, and since Lucy doesn't go to Peyton's school, it might work. Maybe they'll click. Maybe—"

"And maybe not, Ross. Don't count on anything when it comes to preteen girls. They're at that almost-grown-up stage. Their hormones are raging, and you never know what you'll get." So much for keeping her mouth shut.

Ross studied her in silence. "You're right."

She relaxed her shoulders. "It's hard not having a wife who's gone through all the puberty stuff making it easier to talk with Peyton. Now it's something you'll have to do, I'm afraid."

"I know. I dread it."

She reached over and rested her hand on his. "Let's do this. Make plans with her, and then let me know how she's accepting the idea. Any thought about how you'll celebrate?"

"She wants to have dinner at Benihana." He angled his head. "Been there?"

"No, but I've heard of it. Lucy would enjoy it. All the knife tricks and watching the chefs cook. Plus she loves shrimp."

"Then that settles it."

His silly expression lightened their previous conversation,

but what he said hadn't. Too many things were left unsettled. The more Kelsey thought about Lexie's concern, the more real it became. She didn't need reality. Kelsey longed for a bit of fantasy in her life.

Ross's attention slid from the chef's flashing knife to Lucy's gleeful applause. Peyton had quieted as she sized up their guests. He had no idea what she had on her mind. The girls were opposites. Peyton's dark hair, the color of his and usually tied back in a ponytail, today hung in curls around her shoulders. Lucy's shorter blond waves bounced with her animation. She spoke well and directly, not afraid to show her enthusiasm while Peyton's personality had slipped into a bottle with a tight cork. The situation disappointed him.

Peyton's attitude didn't help her relationship with Lucy, either. He overheard Lucy ask her mother why Peyton was so unfriendly. Ross slithered into silence, his frustration roping him in knots. Before he sank deeper, he refocused on the chef as he set out the sauces for the meat and shrimp.

Frustration turned to guilt. He'd noticed Peyton watching Lucy and her mother with longing written on her face. She missed her mom. She'd been six, and the loss had overwhelmed them both. How could he be a mother, too? He leaned closer to Peyton. "Did you like the soup and salad?"

She shrugged. "It was good."

"Look there." He motioned to the grill. "Here comes your favorite."

She eyed the shrimp. "I like steak better."

Pressing his lips closed, Ross gave up. When she was in a snit, nothing pleased her.

The chef stood over the scorching griddle, juggling his spatulas, flipping severed shrimp tails into his tall hat, then flicking a grilled shrimp onto Lucy's plate. Her eyes as blue as her mother's opened wide while she giggled and attempted to pick up the shrimp with chopsticks. It fell, but she only laughed and tried again.

The chef glided past them, mounding the shrimp appetizer onto each attractive dish before he pulled out a knife the size of a machete and chopped and grilled zucchini and bean sprouts.

"Dad, why didn't he flick a shrimp onto my plate?"

Ross's heart constricted, hearing Peyton's disappointed voice. "We're not finished eating yet, sweetie, and Lucy is clapping and showing her appreciation. Maybe that's why he picked her."

"But it's *my* birthday." She lifted her shoulders up to her ears and let them fall.

His frustration and guilt multiplied. Despite her illness, Peyton had to learn that she still had to deal with people of all kinds. He'd tried to teach her that showing appreciation encouraged people to respond in a positive way. Sometimes he even cringed at her lack of gratitude when he went out of his way to show her his love in a special way. Weighted with helplessness, Ross wondered if Peyton would have been different if Ruthie had lived.

The evening hadn't started out well. When the hostess seated them, he had tried to manipulate Peyton in the middle beside Lucy, but she withdrew and sat beside him on the end. Kelsey took the seat next to him while Lucy sat on the other end—two girls like bookends. He hoped Peyton would brighten at their next stop, a surprise he thought she'd enjoy.

Having Kelsey beside him reminded him how nice it was to be a couple. They laughed and chatted like old friends, and he had a difficult time realizing they'd only met a short time ago. She fit into his life, and if the girls became friends, she could likely become a good friend. When he gazed at her profile, his pulse tripped. Connecting with a woman in such a natural way turned his life around. Ross spent his days concentrating on and worrying about Peyton, and Kelsey had become a needed distraction. A beautiful and amazing distraction.

She angled his way, her eyes catching his, and his pulse did more than trip. He hoped nothing went wrong with their friendship, but he'd prayed for his wife and for Peyton, too. God seemed to pick and choose which prayers He would answer.

The chef's eyes caught his, and he leaned closer. "Is this the birthday girl?"

Ross nodded, and the man gave him a subtle wink.

Along with the other vegetables, the chef had placed thick slices of onion on the huge griddle, and while he chopped some of them, he allowed a few to grill. Within moments, he began selecting the onion rings from large to smaller, forming a cone. Lucy craned her neck to watch, and he nudged Peyton. "I think he's doing this for you."

She gazed up at him, her hazel eyes brighter than they'd been.

They watched him pour a liquid into the center of the rings and then turn to Peyton. "We don't have birthday candles, but I've made you a birthday volcano." He struck a match, held it over the center of the cone and a large flame shot from the top. Everyone at the table oohed, and Kelsey broke into the happy-birthday song. He and Lucy joined in, along with the chef and strangers sitting at their table surrounding the grill. Peyton beamed at the special attention, and it did his heart good.

She hadn't said thank you, but she'd smiled, and the chef smiled back as he went from plate to plate with the vegetables before he prepared the meat.

Lucy leaned across her mother. "That was neat. Better than a birthday cake, right, Peyton?"

Peyton only nodded.

Lucy settled back in her chair, and Ross sent up a prayer

that the Lord intervene in a big way as the evening went on, or tonight could be a total bust.

Kelsey watched the girls moving from exhibit to exhibit, delving into every hands-on physics experiment they ran across. Never having visited the Cranbrook Institute of Science, now she wished she'd brought Lucy here before. The place amazed her and delighted Lucy.

As the girls examined the equipment, learning how matter works, she'd found a bench and rested her feet. For some dumb reason, she'd worn pumps. But then dinner meant sitting. She grinned, recalling that Ross had stressed that the evening wouldn't end with their meal.

As always, Lucy's curiosity whetted her appetite not to miss a thing. She'd taken in all of the Cape Farewell exhibit, and wherever they went, Lucy had tried to engage Peyton, but the girl who rarely smiled seemed to withdraw into herself the more Lucy tried. Lucy's disappointment showed, and Kelsey's heart wrenched for Peyton as well as Ross. He'd tried so hard to engross her in conversation with Lucy numerous times without success.

Though the evening hadn't been a disaster, Ross had obviously hoped for much more. Kelsey beckoned to him, seeing stress growing on his face.

He sidled next to her and released a lengthy sigh. "Sorry about the evening. As I said, Peyton has her moody times, and today seems to be one of them."

"You've given her a great birthday celebration so don't beat yourself up."

"I know, but—"

She touched his arm. "Was it us? Is she distant because we're here?"

He patted the back of her hand. "I really don't think so. At home she's often the same way. She stays in her room." He pursed his lips, as if trying to bottle his emotions. "I don't know what to do anymore."

She lifted her other hand and covered his, wishing she had Solomon's wisdom. "Have you discussed Peyton's behavior with her? You said some very meaningful things when you told me about her problems." She lifted her hand and pressed it against his cheek, seeing his good looks tense with disappointment. "Think of times you've been rebuffed or you felt out of it in a crowd. It's so easy to step back so you won't experience those feelings again. We protect ourselves that way." She lowered her hand. "Maybe Peyton doesn't understand why she feels the way she does."

"It's a defense mechanism, one we all use at times." He rubbed his temple. "But if she never tries, she'll never realize that she can make friends."

His eyes captured hers with a desperate look that tore at her heart.

"She needs a woman's love, and though my mom is so good to Peyton, that's about all the female contact she has. I have no siblings, so Peyton has no aunts or cousins. It's tragic in a way."

Her mind spun. "I see why you're frustrated."

"If she'd give you and Lucy a chance, you could make a difference for her." He closed his eyes and shook his head.

His comment jolted her. Was that what the friendship meant to him? She tried to let the thought slip from her mind but couldn't. "I'm not sure I like—"

Ross's eyes bolted open. "What I said was crude. Please don't think that I'm befriending you only because of Peyton."

Though she weighed her words, Kelsey let them fly. "I wondered." Better to end the friendship now, than to be hurt.

He shifted on the bench to face her. "Can I be honest?"

"I'd like that more than anything."

"I'm not good at this, but I'll try to explain. I like you. Really like you. You're a beautiful woman, but you mean more to me than what's on the outside. I like your common sense. I like your bravery. When we're not stressed, you make me laugh."

"You've given me a few chuckles, too." A strong need to lighten the moment struck Kelsey. He'd been through enough today.

"Let me finish. I haven't had a social life since Ruthie died. First I wasn't ready, and then Peyton was diagnosed—"

"What happened to your wife? Are you divor—"

"She died."

Died. The word sank to Kelsey's stomach.

"She died from cardiomyopathy. The same disease Peyton has."

She gasped. The news struck her hard. "Ross, that's too much for anyone. No wonder you're struggling."

"Peyton's illness was caught sooner. I recognized the symptoms, and though I tried to pretend they weren't there, I faced it. We have hope with Peyton. God willing, lots of hope."

Kelsey captured his hands in hers. "I'll pray for you and Peyton every day. I realize we're new friends, but I'm sick at heart learning this."

"To be honest, I hate to tell people. I don't want sympathy or pity. I'm strong and capable."

"You are. I can see that, but you can accept people's understanding."

His head bobbed in agreement. "That's important."

"Mom, did you see what I did with that ball?" Lucy bounded to their sides, pointing at one of the experiments.

"No, I'm sorry. I missed what you did." She glanced at Ross, sensing that their conversation had stopped at a bad time.

Lucy beckoned to her. "I'll show you."

Ross rose as he checked his watch. "I have one more surprise for you girls."

Lucy bounced on her toes. "Another surprise?"

His valiant effort to stay positive warmed Kelsey's heart.

"We're going to see a show called Space Park in the planetarium. It's 3-D projections choreographed to music." He rose and swiveled around, searching for Peyton. When she glanced his way, he waved to her. "We should get in line or we'll miss it."

"Speaking of missing it…" Kelsey opened her purse. "We have a present for Peyton."

Peyton arrived in time to hear her, and a glint of interest flashed in her eyes. "A present?"

"Yes, a birthday present." Kelsey eyed Ross. "Do we have one minute?"

He nodded as she dug into her bag and pulled out a small, gift-wrapped box. She handed it to Peyton. "Happy birthday."

Lucy snuggled in beside her. "I hope you like it."

Peyton tore off the paper, and Kelsey stooped and cleared it from the floor, along with the ribbon, while Peyton opened the lid and looked inside. "Daddy." She held it up.

He grasped the box and looked inside. "That's your birthstone. Amethyst. It's beautiful."

He returned it to her. "Would you like to wear it?"

She nodded, and he unhooked the heart-shaped pendant from the flaps and fastened it around her neck. "It's a heart for Valentine's day."

Lucy peered at it. "It's pretty." She eyed Kelsey. "I'd like a birthstone, too."

"Yours would be different, though."

Peyton's comment surprised Kelsey. "She's right, Lucy. Your birthstone is sapphire."

Lucy looked puzzled.

"That's a bright blue." Kelsey looked around the room for something that color.

"Sapphire like your eyes." Ross tilted Lucy's chin and grinned. "The same as your mom's."

Kelsey's pulse fluttered.

"Sapphire." Lucy peered into her mother's eyes. "I love blue."

Peyton fingered her necklace. "I like purple."

Ross jumped in. "Well, I like purple and blue."

Kelsey gave him a poke, hearing sarcasm in his voice. She feared that he had had enough. "What did your daddy give you for your birthday?" A new topic was in order.

"Three books to add to my Nancy Drew collection and a gift card for Macy's for some new clothes."

Lucy leaned against Kelsey. "Mom, I need some new clothes."

Her expression disappointed Kelsey. Lucy rarely showed envy as she did tonight. Instead of a comment, she gazed at her watch.

"We'd better get in line or we'll miss the show," Ross said.

She followed Ross, but her mind stayed with her worry— the girls' competition. Purple. Blue. Maybe rivalry was natural. Lucy sometimes butted heads with Cooper, but two girls the same age should have a few things in common. These two seemed to be at opposite ends of the spectrum.

Ross would do anything for Peyton. She would do anything for Lucy. So where did that leave her and Ross? At opposite ends, too?

Chapter Four

Kelsey's spine knotted with anticipation, waiting to open the MOSK meeting. She pushed back her shoulders and pulled them forward, hoping to relieve the stress. Despite reservations, she'd settled her mind to her mission. She had to, now that she'd met Ross and understood his need.

Her gaze drifted over the women, recalculating a way to approach the topic without laying too much out in the open. She'd almost hoped Lexie wouldn't attend, because she knew too much about the situation, and Kelsey knew she'd feel guilty if she didn't put everything on the table. Facts, feelings and familiarity. Maybe that was the problem. Being too close to Ross and her roiling emotions may have undermined her wisdom and skewed her ability to see all sides of the issue.

The clock hand ticked past the hour, and a couple of women eyed their watches. She had to begin. The agenda gave her time to think through her points, and she hoped by the end of their sharing time, she would have the right words.

Kelsey clapped her hands together and managed a grin. "I'm glad to see so many of you here today. We have some things to talk about, but first, we begin by sharing." She shifted her gaze to the back of the room. "I see a couple of visitors with us. Welcome. If you have questions, please ask.

We're here to support each other in any way we can. Now—"
she gestured toward the seating arrangement "—let's scoot
our chairs around to form a circle today. It's nice when we
can see everyone."

The women shifted—some standing and moving their
seats and others wiggling their chairs into position. When
they'd formed a ragged circle, she turned to Ava.

"Ava, why don't you start? Tell us about your week, and
introduce yourself to our guests."

Ava raised her hand with a wave, as if wanting to make
sure everyone knew who she was, and began. "I'm Ava
Darnell, a single mom. My son, Brandon, has Hodgkin's lym-
phoma. He's fourteen." She gazed at the women in the back
of the room as muffled sounds of compassion rippled toward
her. "We had good news this week. This round, we had an
excellent report. His blood tests showed a little improvement,
and he has more energy than he's had in a long time."

Words of assurance echoed through the room before the
next mom began her news, but Kelsey's attention slipped into
her thoughts and the voices faded. Though she tried to focus,
she was concentrating on her goal for the meeting.

Ross's image had rattled through her mind since Peyton's birthday. He wanted so much for his daughter, but until
Peyton was willing to give and take a chance, Ross's hopes
would never come to fruition. Ideas kept coming, but how
could she step in and influence changes? Her actions would
result in resentment from Peyton and Ross. She would make
Ross feel like a failure as a dad, and he wasn't. Ross gave so
much. She saw it in his face and his actions. He tried so hard
it broke her heart.

Lucy's disappointment made her sad, too. She'd wanted
her to be friends with Peyton, but the girl didn't budge toward
acceptance at all. She'd reacted the opposite and thwarted
everyone's efforts to extend her a happy birthday. Kelsey refused to put Lucy through that again.

But then she envisioned Peyton. Lonely. Lost. Forlorn. An ache flared in Kelsey's chest. She would talk with Lucy and explain. Lucy could take it. She was strong and kind.

Kelsey's attention snapped back to the women. She'd missed the guests' introductions, and guilt assailed her. A moderator needed to focus and be on top of things. She rose and managed a pleasant smile. "Thanks everyone for sharing from your heart, especially our visitors." She scanned the faces. "Did we miss anyone?" She would have known had she paid attention.

Blank looks stared back. She'd goofed. "I mean, do we have any other thoughts?"

Some heads nodded no. Others swiveled to scan the room.

"Then, it's time to move on. We have two topics today. One has to do with a fundraiser we'd like to sponsor to help our members who are having financial problems. The other is one I'd like to bring up…again."

Expressions changed when she added *again*.

"So let me offer this now as food for thought." She lifted her shoulders and dragged in a lengthy breath. "A while ago we voted on whether we should allow men to join this organization. Most of us are single parents, but some are married. The consensus was that men want to 'do' rather than 'talk.' Most of us agreed."

Heads nodded and rumblings of examples buzzed among them.

"That's why I'm here," one of the guests said. "My husband puts his head in the sand. He doesn't want to face what our daughter is going through. He deals with the information but not the pain we're all feeling."

Kelsey nodded, wishing someone would come up with an illustration to support a man's need to be open. "That's what we agreed on." Ross's words filled her mind. "But recently I've met a man who is interested in a support group, and ours fits his time, schedule and location. I challenged him with the same things you're saying. Men don't want to talk about their feelings. They want action. They want to do something. And his response took the wind out of me." She surveyed the room, hoping her next words would touch them as they had her. "He said that when a man has a sick child there's little he can do."

An intake of breath dotted the room. Some women squirmed, gazing at the ceiling or the floor, anywhere but at each other. "He said more. He said it's hard to open up, but he thought he would benefit from hearing others' struggles and knowing he's not alone. And he thought he could learn from others' experiences."

Ava jumped in. "We do learn from each other's situations. It's taught me how to handle my grief and what to be grateful for. It's easy to forget the good when we're dealing with so much bad."

Kelsey wanted to hug Ava. "I voted against men, too, but I've seen a different side of it now, and I realize that many single men have no one to talk with. They can't show their feelings to their friends or coworkers because they don't want to look weak. Where can they turn?"

"To groups like this."

Lexie's voice surprised her.

"Sorry, I'm late." She pulled her shoulder from the door-frame and stepped into the room. "I've thought about this lately, too. Originally I was against it, but my feelings have changed since I met the man Kelsey's talking about. And I'm sure he's not the only one. We're all parents. We love our kids whether we're fathers or mothers. We all need support."

"Thanks, Lexie." Kelsey's heart surged with her friend's encouragement. "I'm not asking you to vote today. But I'm asking you to think about it during the week. Put yourself in a father's position, and we'll vote on it next week. Decide with your heart what's best for all of us dealing with seriously ill children."

Her hands trembled as she lowered them to her sides. "Now, let's hear about the fundraiser idea." She slipped into a chair, waiting for the tension to fade. Nothing would please her more than to tell Ross the group had opened the door to him and other men who loved their sick kids and needed support. *Lord, please, give us an answer. If it's not our door, open another one. Help us to show compassion.*

Ross stood outside Ethan's office door, grasping for courage to open it and talk. He liked Kelsey more than he wanted to admit, but his brain told him he was heading for trouble. But how could he explain it to Ethan and make sense? Ethan's situation was different. Lexie's boy had been fighting leukemia. Ethan supported her and Cooper without shortchanging his own child, since he had none. No conflict of interest there.

Ethan's telephone receiver clicked as he hung up, and Ross stepped forward. Ethan's back was to the door, but when he heard Ross's steps, he swiveled around. "Hey, how's it going?"

"Fine." Not fine, but no one expected a truthful answer. "Am I interrupting?"

He brushed his hand in the air. "No. I have to make changes to some plans. The family can't afford everything they want." He shrugged. "We'll do it in stages, I guess."

Ross understood that problem. "Do you mind if I sit?"

Ethan's eyebrows raised. "Not at all." He tilted back in his chair. "Something wrong?"

Ross flicked his head, looking for words.

"Job or personal life?"

"Personal?"

The word caused Ethan to lean forward, placing his folded hands on his desk. "I hope you and Kelsey haven't—"

"Nothing quite like that. We get along great." He pressed his dry lips together. "It's…"

"Have you seen her?"

"Yes." The memory sank to the pit of his stomach.

"I mean on a date?"

"Sort of. We went out for Peyton's birthday. Lucy and Kelsey. Dinner and we went to the Cranbrook Institute of Science. They have all kinds of hands-on things for kids, plus a laser show."

Ethan studied his face. "It didn't go well? I mean with the girls?"

"Not as well as I'd hoped. Peyton wasn't receptive. Things were tense." Things were horrible.

"Peyton's relationships have been limited, Ross. You can't expect wonders. At least not that fast."

"I know. I hoped. But I'm thinking and…" Ethan's serious expression motivated him to spit out his concern. "I really like Kelsey. A lot. But my life belongs to Peyton, and I—"

"Ethan, your life doesn't belong to Peyton. It's yours. You give her your full attention because you love her. But you're good at multitasking. You have to be as a contractor. Find ways to split your time, and you'll be better for it."

"Better for it? What do you mean?"

"It's like anything in life. If you keep your eyes aimed at one thing, you miss other important things. When you let your time and interest take in more, you're a more complete person. You can't cut off the joy of life and dwell on Peyton's illness. You'll be a sad, depressed person and that's not good for you or her."

The words cut him. "Is that what I am? Sad and depressed?"

"I didn't mean it like that. I'm talking feelings." He rose from the chair and rounded his desk. "We don't talk about feelings much, but they drive us. Emotions cause us to react in certain ways and believe certain things. When they're one-sided, we're not getting the full picture. I lived my wife's death over and over, and never opened myself to anything beyond that until Lexie came into my life."

"That's why I came to you, I suppose."

Ethan leaned against his desk, resting a hand on the top. "Do you like Kelsey enough to work at it? You can learn how to share time, and maybe Lucy and Peyton could become friends. They both—"

"That's the problem. Peyton won't let it happen."

"Ahh." Ethan slipped onto the desktop and leaned forward. "So that's it." A frown settled on his face. "And they've only been together once, right?"

He nodded.

Ethan flung his hands upward. "You've said Peyton struggles with friendships at school. She hasn't clicked with the kids. You know how people are. She's not trusting yet. Give her time. Plan another event."

"I'm not sure Lucy will want to spend time with her again."

"Don't look for problems. Lucy's a great kid. She and Cooper are friends, and they go at each other when it comes to games. Lucy's determined to win, but they're still buddies. It may take a while for the girls to bond. Lucy and Cooper have been friends since Lexie met Kelsey. That was some time ago."

Ross tried to digest what Ethan was saying. He made some good points. "I need to think of something that's nonthreatening or competitive."

"How about going to a movie and afterward stopping for ice cream? They'll be together but nothing challenging. No need for a lot of conversation."

Ross chuckled. "Unless it's picking out a movie."

"Okay, but you can always put ideas in a hat and let them draw. Then it's no one's idea."

Ethan's good humor gave Ross hope. He grinned as he rose. "Great idea. Thanks."

"Anytime." Ethan slippedd from the desk and slid his arm around Ross's shoulders. "I suppose Kelsey told you I was irked at Lexie when she advised her not to get too involved with you."

His back tightened. "No, she didn't."

"Oops." His arm dropped to his side. "I assumed she did. Lexie feared exactly what you're talking about. How can two people with sick kids find time for another person?"

Ross nodded his head. At least he wasn't the only one to question the situation.

"But I saw it differently. I think the two of you deserve some fun and companionship other than with your kids." He squeezed Ross's shoulder. "For the reasons I mentioned."

"Thanks for the vote of confidence." He extended his hand and Ethan gave it a squeeze.

When he stepped into the hallway, though a weight remained on his shoulders, his step felt lighter.

"What do you think about the movie idea?"

Kelsey gazed at Ross's eyes filled with hope. Her chest constricted, thinking of the pleading she would have to do. "Let me check with Lucy, okay?"

His head lowered as if studying the carpet of her living room. "I understand. If I were Lucy, I wouldn't want to spend time with Peyton, either."

"Ross." She reached across the space and grasped his hand. "Peyton's a sweet girl, but she's been rejected so often she's put up barriers. Even adults do that."

He nodded, but the discouraged look remained on his face. "I'm baffled." His pleading gaze searched hers. "I've talked with her and tried to explain that she has to reach out to people. She can't."

"She can. It takes time. Everything's in God's time. I've heard you say that yourself."

A grin crept to his lips. "Easy to say but hard to follow."

"I know, but trust. Friendships take time to build." Her pulse skipped. Some friendships never happened. They both knew that. "Let me see what Lucy says."

She strode to the doorway and down the short hallway to Lucy's bedroom. "Can I come in?" She tapped on the door.

The door swung open. "I'm doing homework."

She rested her hand on Lucy's shoulder and kissed her cheek. "You're my A-1 daughter."

Lucy rolled her eyes. "I'm your only daughter, Mom."

"But if I had two, you'd be my A-1."

Her nose wrinkled but a grin appeared. "Is Ross here?"

"He is." She motioned toward the room, and Lucy stepped aside for her to enter. When Lucy faced her, Kelsey closed the door. "Ross wondered if you'd be willing to go to a movie with them."

"*Them* meaning him and Peyton?"

"No, all of us. A movie and maybe ice cream after?" Kelsey managed not to smile when Lucy's face lit up. Ice cream was her favorite treat.

"Which movie?"

Kelsey stared at the ceiling. "It's…the one with Emma Roberts. You should enjoy it. I think it's a suspense or something."

Lucy shrugged. "You really want me to do this?"

She nodded. "Peyton needs approval." She raised her hand to stop Lucy's comment. "I know it's not easy, but be compassionate. She has a very nice dad so I'm sure she's a nice girl."

Lucy raised her eyebrows.

"With a few problems."

Eyebrows lowering, Lucy gave a nod. "I know." She drew up her shoulders. "When?"

"Tonight. It's Friday. No school tomorrow. And remember. Ice cream."

"Okay, Mom. But that wasn't fair."

Kelsey chuckled. "I know. But the ice cream was Ross's idea not mine." She headed for the door and pulled it open. "Finish what you're doing and get ready. I'll tell Ross."

After she closed the bedroom door, she leaned against the wall, hoping to discard the random thoughts charging through her head. All of them involved Ross. Where could this relationship lead? And what kind of relationship did Ross intend? Since Lexie's wedding, their meetings had been like playdates—parents taking their kids to the local park to ride the slides and swings. Is that all it was? If so, did she want that kind of acquaintance?

Sometimes her heart skipped a beat when she pictured Ross. The idea added excitement to her life and stirred her awareness to realize that romance might feel good in her life if she could learn to trust again. Ross had become a faithful friend. His devotion to Peyton, even the love he still held for his wife, registered a good feeling in Kelsey. Yet the relationship lacked too much. Two people needed time to develop a solid friendship before it grew into something more. But already her heart had gotten tangled up in the situation. Was it feelings for Ross or Peyton? When she closed her eyes, his face appeared—not his daughter's.

She pushed herself from the wall, her stride slower than when she left. Guarding her heart needed to be a priority. Nothing should distract her from Lucy's needs, both as her only parent and as a caregiver. Thankfulness for Lucy's recent health billowed in her mind. Lucy had been well for months. She thanked God for the blessing.

When she entered the living room, Ross's head snapped up, his eyes searching hers. She nodded. "It's fine." She approached him and sank into the chair she'd vacated. "Have you talked with Peyton?"

"I did before I left. I'll call Mrs. Withers. She's with Peyton and will tell her to get ready."

"Would you like some coffee? I have a pot made."

"Thanks. That sounds good."

He pulled his cell phone out of his pocket as Kelsey headed for the kitchen. The dishwasher from the dinner dishes had grown silent. She opened the door but closed it again. Ross didn't need that much time for his call and she would put the dishes away later. Instead, she poured coffee into two cups, and when she carried them back into the living room, Ross's call had ended.

"Thanks." He grasped the cup and rested his back against the chair. "She'll be ready when we get there." He took a careful sip of the hot coffee.

"Lucy's finishing her math, and then we can go." Their conversation had become stilted. She eyed Ross to see if he noticed, then decided it was her problem. Too much thinking. Like too much salt, that could ruin the soup, except in this case, the soup was her confusing relationship with him. She tasted the coffee and set the cup down.

"Do you ever wonder if you're overindulgent with Peyton?" The question flew from her mouth like a disturbed bat and it was just as frightening when she heard the words.

Ross's eyes widened and confusion registered on his face. "Do you think I am?" He gripped the cup as if it were a lifesaver.

Yes. Maybe. She didn't know, but that wasn't the question she meant to ask. "I think I've babied Lucy too much sometimes. I just wondered if you ever think that."

Coffee sloshed from the cup to his leg but went unnoticed as he peered at her. "How can you overindulge a sick child?"

Irritation tinged his words, and Kelsey wished she hadn't said it that way. "What I mean is, do we hover over them? Are we allowing our kids to learn to fend for themselves? They're becoming teenagers, and they—"

"Kelsey." He set the cup on the table. "I don't know if Peyton will ever be a teenager. Her mother only lived a couple years after she was diagnosed. It was too late."

A deep ache ripped through Kelsey's heart. She hung her head and closed her eyes, sensing his pain not only for himself but for his daughter. "How long ago, Ross? Does Peyton remember her mom?"

"She was six, and she remembers."

The sorrow in his voice enveloped her. "You're trying to be mother and father, I know."

"And I'm not good at either one."

Her head shot up. "Don't say that. I wasn't accusing you when I asked that question about overindulging." Dumb, stupid question. She wished she could bite back the words. "I was asking because of my own guilt, too. We forget our kids that have to survive in the real world. Let's be optimistic and believe that both of our kids will be teenagers and adults. Let's do that."

Ross drew in a ragged breath. "I tell myself that every day."

"Believe it every day. That's how we hold on. Prayer and hope. I live with both on my heart and lips."

"Sorry for jumping at you, Kelsey. I feel guilty sometimes. I don't know how to ease up and force issues with Peyton. I don't know how to stop myself from giving in. She has me wrapped around her finger, I suppose."

"We're all guilty of that." She managed to grin. "You know about tough love. It's sort of like that, I guess, but we have to use it on ourselves. Not the kids."

A noise alerted her, and she glanced toward the doorway. "You're ready?"

Lucy nodded, her gaze drifting to Ross.

He grinned. "Ready for a movie and a treat?"

She gave him a playful look. "Ice cream. I'm ready for that."

"Okay, then. Let's go." He rose and beckoned them toward the door.

Kelsey gazed at her daughter, her pride growing. Lucy

handled things well. Now if they could only help Peyton learn how to manage just as well. The thought wavered in her mind. Hope, she reminded herself. Hope and prayer.

Chapter Five

Ross focused his eyes on the menu while his attention hung on the girls. They had been courteous to each other but distant. Conversation had been minimal.

"Did you enjoy the movie?"

Kelsey's voice entered his concentration.

"I figured out the mystery." Lucy tossed her blond curls. "But then I'm good at puzzles."

Peyton stared at the menu though her glance didn't go unnoticed. Ross suspected that she was looking for some kind of comeback, but nothing came. "What looks good, Peyton?" he asked.

She gave a bored shrug before looking up. "A sundae, maybe."

"With whipped cream?" Lucy ran her tongue over her lips.

A faint look of interest crossed Peyton's face. "With a cherry on top."

"Me, too. I love the cherries."

Ross swung his gaze from Lucy to Peyton. They'd agreed on something. Even a cherry seemed like a victory. "How about sundaes all around?"

Everyone nodded as tension slipped from his shoulders. He eyed the waitress, and she gave a nod before heading their way. "That was easy." She grinned, collecting the menus. "Four chocolate and vanilla sundaes with hot fudge, whipped cream and a cherry on top. Two decafs and two waters." He turned to the girls. "Are you sure that's all you want?"

They both nodded, a look on their faces that let him know they were surprised they'd agreed on two things while at the restaurant.

While eating the ice cream, their conversation dwindled. Spoons clinked against the glass goblets and napkins rustled as they wiped their mouths. The hot fudge dripped from Ross's spoon and he caught the sweet syrup with his tongue, his spirit lifting as he gazed at the three females around the table.

Peyton and Lucy saved their cherries until near the end and, eyeing each other, they lifted them, dangled the red orb by the stem and dropped them into their mouths with a giggle. The sound reverberated like beautiful music. Ross's hopes soared. Hope and prayer. Kelsey had said it earlier that day, and she'd spoken the truth.

Once the girls had finished and the waitress had refilled their coffee cups, Lucy slipped from her chair, her eyes pleading. "Can I have some money to play arcade games?" she asked her mom.

Kelsey looked at Peyton and then she glanced at Ross, her lips pursed. "What about—"

"Peyton, do you want to play, too?" Ross sensed that he'd saved the day, and Peyton's grin finalized the situation. He reached in his wallet and dug out a couple of dollars.

Lucy had her money in hand and dashed off, and when Peyton closed her hand around the bills, she darted off, too.

Concern shot through Ross. Lucy embodied energy—a bundle of vigor not easily quelled. But Peyton. He drew in a breath. She needed to be careful. Her energy levels were limited at times. Putting the two together could be like water vapor mixing with low atmospheric pressure creating a hurricane. Disaster. Peyton could never keep up with Lucy.

Kelsey's attention focused on the girls until she turned toward him. "What do you think?"

A grin stole over his face. "I see promise."

"So do I." She reached across and rested her hand on his. "Slow but sure. That's the best way. Let them move at their own pace. We can't engineer it."

Pace. Anxiety skittered across his chest. "Lucy's a bundle of energy, isn't she?"

"She was down for so long that now she's trying to make up for lost time. I'm thrilled seeing her so bubbly and excited about everything." She shook her head. "I'm afraid I'm a prideful mama. She's my bright little star."

"She is." But that didn't get to the heart of the matter. "That worries me, though."

Her hand slipped from his, a scowl replacing her pleasant expression. "What do you mean?"

"Peyton isn't well yet." Would she ever be? The sundae churned in his stomach. "She can't do all the things Lucy can do. What if—"

Kelsey leaned against the seat back. "Don't look for problems. Kids can be monitored. I can ask Lucy to tone it down, and you can explain to Peyton that she has to be careful. They know their illnesses."

His eyes closed, taking in her words. Would it be that easy? Kids were kids. They competed. "Kids want to do what other kids do. I'm sure you went through that with Lucy."

"I did."

"So it's…" He shrugged. "Difficult. I hate looking Peyton in the face and telling her she can't do things, even though I know it's for her own good."

"Talk to your doctor, Ross. Maybe Peyton can do more than you think."

"Maybe." The hope he'd felt melted into apprehension. He

gazed at Kelsey's thoughtful face. Her long hair fell to her shoulders with only a slight wave, the part that annoyed her still present. She lifted her hand and drew her fingers through her hair as if she realized he was noticing the part.

"You're an attractive woman. I suppose you know that."

Her brows furrowed. "Me?" A quick shake of her head followed. "I'm rather plain, I think, but it's nice to hear you say I'm not too bad-looking."

Not too bad-looking. He wanted to rebut the comment, but he let it slip. "We've both led unique lives, haven't we? When you don't have a partner, it sometimes skews your attitudes."

"Maybe we're more practical then."

"Maybe, but is that what life has to be? What about a little risk? Adventure? Outside the box? Even a little bit wild and crazy?"

Her eyes searched his. "And…?"

"And, I don't know." But he did know so why not say it? "I really enjoy your company. I like you. But we haven't had time to get to know each other well." He swallowed the rush of words charging from him. "Let's do something…alone. Get sitters and spend time together."

"Like a date." A faint grin edged onto her face.

"Okay, a date." He chuckled at his uneasy approach. "Would you go out with me?"

"Is this the wild and crazy thing you were talking about?"

"Not quite, but it could be the beginning of an adventure." His heart raced as if he were standing in line for his first roller-coaster ride. "What do you say?"

"I've been known to put my toe outside the box once or twice."

"Then it's a yes."

A smile filled her face as she nodded.

He slid his hand across the table and slipped it over hers. "We're always talking in small snatches of conversation. It will be nice to start a topic and finish it without being int—"

"Mom."

Lucy's voice caught him off guard, making him laugh. Perfect timing.

Kelsey caught the joke, too, and pinched her lips together to stop herself from chuckling. "What, Lucy?"

"I'm out of money."

Kelsey shrugged as she checked her watch. "That's okay because we're out of time."

Ross understood her hint, but instead of disappointment, for once he rose from the chair with plans. He'd call to set a date and a time, but he had a date with Kelsey. A real date and not a foursome.

The sound of footsteps and shifted chairs filtered through Kelsey's thoughts. She smiled and nodded as if nothing clouded her mind as the vote did today. She couldn't call Ross and tell him again that the vote was a veto. When Lexie walked through the door, her look let Kelsey know that she hadn't hidden a thing from Lexie. If she didn't plant an altogether pleasant expression on her face, Ava would be all over her with questions.

"You okay?" Lexie's voice snapped her to attention.

"Fine. You know it's…"

No words were needed. Lexie knew and supported her decision to change her vote from the last one she'd made. She'd been opposed. Not anymore.

The two new women were back and that lifted her spirit although she had no idea if they were for or against her proposal. When the hands of the clock struck the hour, she stepped to the center and opened the meeting. Today she paid attention to what the members said about their children's prognosis and the families' situations. They applauded with good news and offered hope with the bad.

While the last person spoke, Kelsey calmed herself while being amazed that she cared that much. Before she knew

Ross, she hadn't flinched, voting no to the proposal. Her stomach constricted as she faced the truth. Too often, people didn't care about those they didn't know. Even churches willingly made casseroles for funeral dinners or donated to a church cause, but when it came to giving to the oppressed in other parts of the world or feeding the children of Haiti or India—other countries not predominantly Christian—they closed their eyes.

She tugged her thoughts away from the depressing topic and listened to the final report. "Thanks for sharing all the good news and sad news in your lives. Lucy's doing fine right now, but we've all faced the sorrows that come from the plight of our sick children, and we are in support of each other. If you need a friendly voice, remember—call one of us. Let us help in whatever way we can, and don't forget, prayer is one of those ways."

Hearing her comment startled her. She avoided prayer comments for those who weren't believers, but today she felt the need, and maybe the Lord wanted her to open someone's heart who needed to know that prayer helps. God listens.

How often she forgot that herself.

She pulled up her shoulders and faced them. "Last week I made a proposal. Not a new one, since I'd initiated the idea before, but last week I offered a new way to look at the idea of allowing men to be part of our group." She chuckled. "I suppose that would mean a name change as well."

A few giggles hit her ear.

"Last week I asked you to think about the idea and suggested we vote on it this week." She gazed around the room, trying to get a sense of which way the vote would go. She failed and that made her nervous. "Does anyone want to offer any thoughts on the subject?"

One of the new women, Diane, if Kelsey remembered correctly, raised her hand. She gave the woman a nod.

"I told my husband about this, and he curled up his nose, but later that night after he'd thought about it, he said he might like to attend when he could. He works days, but he has flextime, so he could attend occasionally."

"Wonderful, Diane." She watched the woman's expression and was relieved when she didn't correct her. Diane, she said the name over in her mind. "Anyone else?"

Shirley Jack Meyer, one of the regulars, gave a wave. "My husband said he wouldn't come to a meeting like this if you paid him a million dollars."

A couple women chuckled.

Kelsey's heart sank. "I'm sure some husbands wouldn't want to attend…or couldn't because of work, but I'm pleased you told him about it."

"I'm dating a guy who really loves Timmy, and he sounded like he would come."

The voice came from the back, but Kelsey didn't see whose it was. "Thanks. Naturally, it doesn't have to be husbands. Anyone who wants to share in supporting each other." She drew in a breath. "I think that's what we were missing on the first vote. We weren't looking at the needs of others but only our own. That's a bit selfish, I'm afraid."

She saw a couple of frowns, but they faded. "Anyone else?"

Ava's hand shot up. "I'm still on the fence here."

Kelsey stepped closer and opened her mouth, but closed it. She knew Ava well enough to know she had more to say or ask.

"I'm sympathetic to the situation, but what happens if we agree and then it's a disaster and the whole organization falls apart?"

Another member waved. "Why would it fall apart?"

"Because we're not the same anymore. Men might think our worries are silly. My husband used to—" She looked at the newer ladies. "He died from a coronary thrombosis. He called me a worrywart. He said I always looked for the worst. I thought I was being realistic. Bad things happen. They did to him when he died so young."

Kelsey cringed. She'd talked to Ross about being practical. Realistic. Weren't they the same? But his suggestion to be adventuresome, to take a risk, opened the door to a real date. Practicality had its merit but she had to admit that risk taking could also be exciting.

Diane raised her hand. "Look at us here, though. We have different opinions, but we still care about each other. We still support each other. That's why I came back to this group. I didn't expect everyone to agree all the time. And some will never participate, but that's okay."

The comment struck another chord with Kelsey. She and Ross wouldn't agree all the time. That was reality. But they still supported each other and cared about their girls. The idea washed over her like a warm bath. That was comfort. "You're right. We are different and have different needs, but we're comfortable with that, and I think the men would realize that, too, when they saw how we work together."

"Kelsey." Ava stood this time.

She gave a nod. "Go ahead."

"Could we open it to men on a trial basis? Make it clear that if they were uncomfortable—or we were—that they could start their own group?" She motioned to the new woman in the back. "Once men start to come, new ones will join and soon they could become DOSK." She grinned. "Dads of Special Kids."

Voices flew at her. "That will work." "I like that idea." "Let's try it."

For Kelsey, the idea fell flat, but it was better than nothing. "Is this what you want?"

Most nodded while only a few shook their heads. "Then let's put it to a vote."

A few hands shot up. Then others followed. Two people—

including herself—struggled with the yes with an addendum, but the vote passed.

As the women filed out, she pulled her cell phone out of her purse, weighing the urge to call Ross now or wait until he called her about the date.

Date. The word made her feel giddy.

"You're not really happy, are you?" Lexie's hand rested on her shoulder.

"Better than a no vote."

She nodded. "Ross will see it as good news."

Kelsey lifted her hand to show Lexie her cell phone. "I'm going to call him."

"Tell him hello from us." She gave a wave and strode toward the exit.

Kelsey sank into a chair and looked at the phone. She should be smiling, but she felt uneasy. She closed her eyes, opened them and hit the contacts button. Ross's number came in sight, and before she could change her mind, she hit Send. When he answered, air drained from her lungs. After she got out the yes vote, she had to wrap her mind around the condition.

"A trial period?" Ross's voice rose in pitch. "Don't get me wrong, I'm happy but—"

"I know. I feel the same way."

"Thanks, Kelsey. I know that wasn't an easy vote for the ladies. I hope I haven't created a mess for you."

"Don't worry. They'll get used to the idea." She grasped at anything to lighten the mood. "It'll add a little adventure to their lives."

He chuckled. "Speaking of adventure, what about that date?"

Her spirit lifted. "What do you have in mind?"

"This Saturday about 6:30. Dinner at Clawson Steak House, and they have a dance band. We can talk and enjoy the music."

"That sounds nice, Ross. I'll get a sitter, or maybe Lucy can stay with Lexie. I'll check. It works for me."

"Great, and thanks for letting me know about the vote. I'll give you a couple of weeks to adjust and send a warning through you when I'm coming. Maybe I'll pass the test."

She squirmed at the comment. "You've already passed it in my eyes."

They said goodbye, and the conversation flashed through her mind. A test. It sounded uncaring. They created the option as a practical compromise, the same way she'd viewed much of her life. But Ross had offered her an alternative. Take a chance. A smile grew on her face. Dinner and music, and time to talk. The idea slipped through her like satin.

From now on, she would work toward being more open, to look at the less practical side of things, because then she might actually see into someone else's heart.

Ross knotted his tie, looked in the mirror and tugged it off. He studied himself again. A sports shirt and jacket might look better. He shrugged off his dress shirt and suit pants and tossed them on the bed. A first date. How long had it been? Forever, it seemed. He strode to his closet and dug through it. Dark pants? Beige? The temperature had registered only thirty-five degrees. Winter hung over them like an ice pack. He pulled black trousers from a hanger and slipped them on, found a belt and threaded it.

He sank onto the edge of the bed, feeling juvenile. Finally, he pushed himself up and studied his shirts. He settled for a black-and-gray plaid, then tugged a gray pullover from the shelf. He drew it over his head and fixed his collar with shaking fingers. Ross rolled his eyes. He'd enjoyed Kelsey's company on two previous outings. Yes, the girls had been there, but so what? He and Kelsey chatted. They laughed. They got serious, but he enjoyed their time together.

Tonight they'd be alone. That was the only difference.

Alone. That apparently was his problem. He eyed the mirror, giving a nod of approval. Neat but casual. Alone was a bonus. No interruptions. He could learn more about her, and she, about him. Did he even want that? His boring life wouldn't be much to talk about.

He gazed around the small bedroom, picturing Peyton pouting in his master bedroom. Although the decision had been his choice, so often he wished he hadn't given it to her. Kelsey had mentioned spoiling the girls. She called it over-indulgent. He wanted to deny it, but now he asked himself the same question. Peyton had a serious heart condition, but the guestroom would have been plenty of space with a twin bed. A chair and desk would fit on the side wall. The feature that had triggered his decision caught his eye—the double door leading to the porch. The last vestiges of light spilled onto the carpet unhampered by the now leafless trees.

Ross opened his door and strode into the hallway and through the great room. He checked his watch. Mrs. Withers would arrive any minute. When he reached Peyton's door, he paused, then tapped. "Can I come in?"

No response, but the door opened seconds later, and he was greeted by Peyton's unhappy expression. "Why can't I go with you?"

His chest knotted. "You're with me most of the time, except when you're in school."

"Why can't I go with you tonight?"

He wanted to sit with her and talk, but she wasn't budging from the doorway. The room taunted him with his unwise decision. The large space had made her too comfortable with her own easy chair, a TV and a CD player. He'd even set up a desk for her to do schoolwork.

"Sometimes adults need time for adult talk."

"I'm an adult, Dad. You keep forgetting."

"You'll be a teenager soon, Peyton, but I'm going to take time for me tonight." *Kelsey and me.* His pulse skipped.

Trembling. Charging pulse. He shook his head and licked his dry lips. "Don't make me feel guilty for wanting a little time for myself. I give you—" Don't say it. "I love you so much. That will never change."

"You'd rather be with her."

Air flew from his lungs. "I'm with you all the time, Peyton. You're not alone. Lucy has a sitter, too." And he couldn't imagine Lucy whining about it.

The doorbell saved him from Peyton's unhappiness. He bent and kissed her cheek. "Mrs. Withers will order pizza for you. She said she'd make a salad, too."

"Lucky me." The door banged.

Irritation slammed against him. He turned from the door and headed for the foyer, determined to have a pleasant evening despite Peyton's dispirited attitude.

Yet, the door's thud rang in his head.

Chapter Six

When Kelsey pulled open the door, Ross gave her a long look while his pulse skipped up his arm.

She stepped back. "Come in a minute."

"You look amazing." Gorgeous. Her wine-colored dress wrapped around her and draped over her hips in a soft swirl. She'd done something to her hair, and tonight it fell in soft waves to her shoulders. Earrings dangled from her earlobes, and he couldn't take his eyes off them and her beautiful eyes.

Kelsey gazed down at her dress, then searched his eyes. "Thanks." A grin crept to her face, and she ran her fingers over the lapel of his sport coat. "You don't look bad yourself."

He stepped into the foyer, and she closed the door. Her comment echoed in his mind, and he gave a nervous chuckle. "Thanks." When she looked away, he cringed at his ridiculous jitters.

Kelsey motioned toward the living room, and he followed her, seeing an elderly woman in the kitchen doorway.

"Ross, this is Marge Butler. She's my wonderful sitter who only lives down the street."

He crossed to her side and shook her hand.

When he looked back, Kelsey was heading into the hallway as her voice sailed back into the room. "Lucy. Ross is here."

In seconds, Lucy came to the living room door and waved. "Hi, Ross. Have fun, and bring Mom home before midnight." She giggled, gave her mom a kiss on the cheek, then beckoned to the sitter. "Let's make hot chocolate." She darted past him toward the kitchen.

Marge chuckled. "I'm sure she has more up her sleeve." With a grin, she followed Lucy, her head wagging like a bobble-head doll.

Ross smiled at the lighthearted spirit in Kelsey's home. She'd been through so much, yet she faced it as if she'd been born to the task. He envied that ability. And Lucy. Her spirit made him smile but ache at the same time.

Kelsey called a goodnight and stepped into the foyer where he held her coat as she shrugged it on.

Outside, Ross backed out of the driveway and headed toward Rochester Road, his thoughts on the past few minutes. "That was easy."

Kelsey glanced his way. "What?"

"No complaints from Lucy. Not one."

"From Lucy?" She chuckled. "She loves having Marge sit with her. They'll play games until her eyelids droop."

A sigh escaped him before he could stop it. He felt her eyes on him.

"Peyton wasn't too happy?"

He wished it had been that easy. "Not happy at all." He told her the story, wishing he hadn't introduced the topic. They'd left her house with plans for a fun evening and he'd put a damper on it with his dilemma.

"Don't feel guilty, Ross. You need time for yourself, too."

"I tried to explain that to her, but—"

"What's sad is Peyton hasn't connected with her school friends." Kelsey's tone had darkened. "I understand why. Lucy missed school, too, and that made it difficult. I still remember those horrible days—panic, doctor visits, hospitals, bandages, and so much fear. It seemed eternal."

His own panic rose. "Listen Kelsey, I'm sorry I—"

She erased his words. "Kids can be alone part of the time. I think it's good for them, but they need stimulation, too. They need to socialize with their peers, not their parents."

"I know, but you've seen her. It's hard for Peyton."

"I know it is."

Dismay rang in her voice, and Ross wished he'd stayed away from the subject. He'd already taken the evening into a direction he hadn't wanted to go.

Kelsey had leaned back, and he remained silent, probing his mind for things to talk about. Many of their conversations revolved around the kids and their problems. He hoped they had more in common than that, but their silence gave him concern.

When the restaurant came into view, Kelsey straightened her back while Ross's shoulders sank in defeat. He'd gone blank, and he had so much he wanted to know about her. He'd realized a few days earlier that he had no idea if she worked and if so, what she did for a living. What were her interests other than Lucy? What had happened to her husband? A multitude of questions now whirled through his mind, and he thanked the Lord for filling his empty head.

Ross swung into the parking lot, glad he'd requested a table far from the band. Not that he wouldn't enjoy the music, but he wanted to spend time with Kelsey. Time without interruption.

The hostess led them to their table and handed them menus, and the next minutes were spent selecting their dinners. When he finished, he set his menu on the table and sipped water a waitress had poured while they were perusing the fare.

Kelsey lifted her eyes from the menu. "Everything looks

good. I can't decide between the veal in lemon sauce with artichokes or the shrimp scampi."

"I've had the veal. It's great."

"That solves my problem. I love artichokes."

Her voice had lightened, and he hoped it stayed that way. It would if he monitored his depressing comments. He had so few people to talk with about Peyton's issues, and he looked forward to airing those feelings at the MOSK meetings...that is, if he passed their test. Bitterness charged through him, and he didn't like the feeling. He'd monitored those emotions, trying to look at their decision in a positive light and to understand why they wanted to test it. Still...

"You're quiet."

Kelsey came into focus. He'd been lost in thought. "I haven't decided between a steak or the steak and shrimp diablo, but I'm leaning toward the filet mignon." That was true, but not what he'd been thinking.

"Are you ready to order?"

The waitress's appearance saved him from further discussion on his silence. He gave the woman their choices, ordered coffee and then leaned back. "I realized the other day I have no idea what you do for a living."

Kelsey's shoulders relaxed. "I manage real-estate rentals. It's a great job for me because I can handle so much of it from home. I have office space at South Oakland Realty, but I'm only there occasionally."

He'd never have suspected. "You mean you take care of the properties."

"Right. If they need a plumber or a repairman, they contact me, and I handle it for the owners."

He slipped his hand over hers. "Our jobs have a few things in common."

"I thought about that. You build residences. I just manage them once people move in."

Ross hoped they had more in common than that. But his

mood had lightened, and that was what he'd hoped. "What do you like to do for fun?"

She blinked. "Fun?"

He watched her think and winced inside. Asked the same question, he'd offer the same response. Fun had escaped him for so long between Ruthie's illness and now Peyton's. The word almost seemed absurd. Yet tonight, even talking about sad things at times, he was having the most fun he'd had in years.

Kelsey finally chuckled. "I guess I have to learn about having fun again. I enjoy shopping, as most women do, but I don't do it often, and when Lucy was ill, I purchased what I could on the internet."

Shopping wasn't a commonality. "Movies? Plays? Concerts?"

"Yes. I enjoy them all. I loved going to plays. When I was younger, I spent numerous nights at Pine Knob—the name changed since then, but the setting's still the same. I loved sitting on the lawn. Springsteen, Bon Jovi. I saw Journey in the rain, but who cared? I had fun anyway."

His heart bounced in his chest, seeing her glowing face. "I might have been there the same night. I saw them in the rain. Do you think…?" The warm summer evening returned, rain spattering from the clouds. "'Don't Stop Believin' and 'Open Arms'—"

"Faithfully."

Kelsey's eyes glistened as they laughed and shared a high-five across the table. Ross's chest constricted with the good feeling that washed over him. "Apparently we like the same music."

"But it's been a long time since I've seen anyone in concert."

His knee jerked with the invitation. "Then we need to see who's in town."

"That would be great, Ross." Her eyes searched his. "Really great."

The waitress arrived with their soup and salads first, and then they settled into the meal. The steak was tender and delicious, served with his favorite, a baked potato, and Kelsey praised the veal dish served with pasta. Though the conversation had lulled, the warmth of their previous talk remained. He'd check the papers to see what artists were in town and pick up some tickets.

When the plates were cleared, the waitress brought over a dessert tray and displayed the great-looking options. Key-lime pie. Chocolate peanut-butter mousse pie. Granny Smith apple pie with ice cream.

Kelsey shook her head. "Just coffee, please."

"I'll have coffee, too, and—" He'd noticed that she'd eyed the crème brulée. "How about one of these and two spoons." He raised his eyebrows and ogled Kelsey.

She laughed. "You're tempting me. Okay, just a bite."

The waitress left, and Ross shifted to a chair adjacent to Kelsey to get a better view of the dance band. The music began as their dessert arrived, and Ross's concentration wasn't on the creamy dessert but on the woman beside him. He longed to hold her in his arms to feel her breath against his cheek.

Years had passed since these sensations had touched him, not even a hint of emotion, but tonight the feelings exploded in his heart. He was walking on a minefield, and each step filled him with anxiety. Was he ready to fall head over heels? Was Kelsey even interested in more than a friendship? And if tragedy struck either one of them, could their relationship survive?

"This is delicious."

Kelsey's comment seeped through his thoughts. "It is." He gave a head toss to the band. "Do you like the music?"

"Nice. I love that song."

"Need You Now" flooded the room. The female singer approached the microphone, the tender music setting Ross's senses on edge. "Would you care to dance?"

She set down her coffee cup and gazed at him. Finally, she gave a slight nod. "It's been years."

"Another thing we have in common." He rose and took her hand, leading her through the tables to the dance floor.

Kelsey moved into his arms as the music swelled, his heart pummeled his chest as they swayed to the music. He moved carefully, his mind digging back to his dancing days years earlier. She moved with him, graceful, light as gossamer in his arms. A sweet scent filled the air, her hair kissed his cheek as they moved to the rhythm.

Since they'd arrived, he and Kelsey had established things in common without talking about the girls or illness or sadness. Music, dancing, concerts, even crème brulée. He longed to be reassured that things in common could be the beginning of something special.

The song ended, but before Ross led her off the dance floor, another slow song began. Her heart stirred when she heard the song, "I Want to Know What Love Is." He drew her closer and they swayed to the music, turning with the rhythm, their hands touching, their arms embracing each other. The lyrics moved her. She needed time to think things over, too. She'd wanted to know what love was. She'd thought once she knew what love was, but it had vanished like smoke. Taking a chance and then losing it again would be more than she could face. She wondered if Ross was listening to the words, too.

She felt his gaze on her, and she looked into his eyes. So many deep thoughts flickered there beneath the chocolate of his eyes. Her fingers glided up his back and brushed the nape of his neck, his hair soft against her hand. A spicy fragrance surrounded him, delicate but stimulating. Being in a man's arms again warmed her like a down quilt. She'd been cold for years, but not tonight.

The song ended and they stood close, rocking to the music in their minds, until the band introduced a lively rock-and-roll tune she enjoyed, but not for dancing. Ross's hand moved down her arm and wove his fingers through hers. As they approached the table, he chuckled. "Cold coffee, I suppose."

She didn't care about the coffee. Instead, she wanted to know more about him, his family, his marriage and— Wrong topic. Keep it light and fun. They'd both had their fill of sorrow.

As Ross pulled out her chair, their waitress appeared with the coffeepot and refilled their cups. Kelsey sat wrapped in the moment, the music, the aromas that drifted past—fresh coffee, pasta at the next table—but the sense that etched in her mind was being held again. She'd nearly forgotten that she was a woman.

Ross gazed at her, his mouth pulling into a grin. "I'll be honest. I wondered if I would remember how to dance. I guess it's like riding a bicycle. You never forget, but then you'd have to verify that."

"You danced very well." Her own concerns rifled through her. "I was afraid I'd be all feet, but we handled it quite well."

His hand slipped over hers. "We did."

His gaze captured hers, and she felt glamorous. Hearing him say she looked amazing earlier tickled her. She'd changed her clothes three times, wanting to find the perfect outfit. Normally she tossed clothes on with no thought. Whatever seemed appropriate and practical. But tonight she hadn't been looking for practical—she wanted to look great. Alluring. Finally, she'd settled on the magenta A-line dress, because she liked the dolman sleeves and it flattered her figure. She could hardly believe that she'd given time to that concern, but she had.

Ross gazed at her in silence. She welcomed the time to

think. The dance made her feel special and she didn't want to lose that feeling, but she had questions. "Are your parents in Michigan?"

"They're in Kansas. That's where I grew up. I met Ruthie in college. I was friends with her brother. She was from Michigan, although her parents moved to Seattle after she died. Her brother lives there. I guess her parents couldn't bear the loss."

As if he could. She cringed. "Do you still see her brother?"

He looked away. "We drifted apart after Ruthie died."

Her stomach knotted. "Then you're pretty much alone here."

"Just Peyton and me."

Peyton and him. An empty feeling settled over her again. She had an older sister, Audrey, who lived in Traverse City. Audrey visited occasionally when she or her husband had business in the area or for a special event, but other than that Kelsey took care of herself, too.

"Where are your parents?"

"My dad retired early and they moved to Tennessee on the Georgia border. They wanted to escape winter."

"Do you see them much?"

She sensed that he wanted to hear that they shared the same situation. "They come up a couple times a year. I used to go there, but when Lucy got sick, I was afraid to go too far away from home." She'd spent the last years being anxious about a lot of things. "If she had an episode when I was down there, I'd be stuck. It made sense to stay close to home."

He looked thoughtful. His mouth twitched as if he wanted to ask a question but he didn't. She wondered why. The silence felt uneasy after their earlier banter. She checked her watch, surprised that they'd been there for nearly three hours.

He must have noticed and looked at his watch. "It's almost ten. I'm surprised. The time flew."

"It did." She lifted the cup and emptied it. "I suppose I should get home."

"Why? You have permission to be out until midnight."

She laughed, recalling Lucy's curfew. "But my fairy god-mother said my carriage would turn into a pumpkin if I didn't leave before midnight."

He gave her a nod. "And I'm guessing Peyton is pacing, waiting for me to get home."

Lucy would be asleep by now, Kelsey guessed.

Ross motioned to the waitress and after he'd settled the bill, they rose and stepped out into the chilly air. Kelsey tilted her head upward. Only a faint glow from the moon's edge tinged the sky, but the stars seemed to glow more brightly.

Ross slipped his arm around her back and guided her to his minivan. When she settled inside, he closed the door. The evening rolled through her mind, the dark moments first but then a lovely ending. Though apprehension hadn't left her, hope grew and wishes multiplied. She could learn to enjoy a man's company again. A taste of it tonight assured her of that.

Ross slipped into the driver's seat and started the engine, but before he shifted into gear, he slipped his hand over hers. "I hope you enjoyed yourself tonight. I know I did."

"It's been really nice. I had a wonderful time."

"Could we do this again? Just the two of us?"

"I think that could be arranged." She warmed with his offer. Yes, she wanted to give this friendship, relationship, whatever it was, a try.

Talk of the girls returned as they drove home. Peyton's attitude and Lucy's exuberance were problems that could be resolved, she hoped. It wasn't fair to Lucy, but she was a good girl and would understand. Peyton seemed old enough to know her limitations.

She gazed at Ross's profile. Classic features fit him, a strong jawline, the hint of a dimple in his cheek, a well-shaped nose and eyes that said more than he did. Dancing, she'd felt the strength of his arms for the first time. His muscles flexed as he maneuvered her across the floor, and his broad back offered her security. He had strength yet a tenderness that embraced her heart.

Pulling herself from her thoughts, Kelsey observed Ross's silence, too. He had been thoughtful as well, and she hoped his thoughts were as inviting as hers. He slowed the minivan and turned onto her street. An unexpected sense of solitude washed over her. She enjoyed his company. "You did nicely, sir." She pointed to her watch. "I'm home before midnight." But spending more time together would have been lovely, too.

"I don't want to offend your timekeeper." He chuckled and opened his door.

"Don't get out. I can manage."

His head drew back, and he arched a brow. "I always walk my dates to the door." He tapped his finger against his temple. "I think I did. It's been a long time."

He made her smile as he slipped out and rounded the minivan to her door.

Kelsey stepped out, feeling Ross's palm against her elbow. His hand slipped to hers as they headed for the porch. Except for a faint glow from the window, stars were their only light on the moonless night. He climbed the steps beside her, and when they paused at the door, her pulse charged up her arm.

Ross's palm brushed her cheek. "We'll do this again."

"I'd enjoy that." Her voice sounded strange, as if someone else were speaking.

His fingers slipped behind her neck, and she stopped breathing as she followed his lips as they drew close to hers. His warm breath swept across her as he lowered his mouth.

Suddenly, the porch light flooded them, and they sprang back as the door opened. "You're home."

Kelsey's heart slipped to her toes as she focused on the

elderly sitter. Her lips tingled with the brief touch of Ross's mouth on hers. "Is everything okay?"

"No problems." Marge's gaze swept past hers, awareness registering on her face. She backed up, her stare swinging from Ross to Kelsey. Her eyes widened and she blinked. "Lucy went to bed a few minutes ago. She wanted to wait up and hear about your evening."

Kelsey managed to grin at Ross. "Isn't that cute?" In the awkward moment, she extended her hand to him. "Thanks for a wonderful time."

His eyes had glazed, a flush of embarrassment on his face, and she was certain her cheeks glowed with mortification.

Ross gave her hand a squeeze. "It was." Another awkward moment slithered past. "I'll call you then."

She nodded.

He backed away and bounded down the steps before turning with a wave. "Soon."

Soon. Yes, she hoped very soon, but at the moment, she wanted to pulverize poor Marge.

Chapter Seven

Ross tossed the magazine onto the table beside him and eyed the wall clock. Disbelieving, he checked his watch. Only fifteen minutes had passed. He'd thought Peyton's tests would be completed a half hour ago. He shifted his focus to the people around him who joined him in their personal waits. Hospitals, doctor's offices, appointments.

Stretching his legs, Ross closed his eyes. As always, the embarrassing evening flew into his mind. Kelsey's lips, so soft, pliant. He'd allowed the kiss to haunt him that evening as they talked, wondering how he could make it happen. He'd envisioned and sensed the delightful touch of her mouth on his. He'd plotted, only to have the vision die like a snapped movie film, leaving only white light on the screen. The porch light.

The question that obsessed him now was Kelsey's reaction. She'd looked uncomfortable. Worse than uncomfortable. Had it been Mrs. Butler and the porch light or the kiss? Naturally, he wouldn't ask her. Not knowing seemed safer.

"Dad."

Ross's head jerked upward. Peyton stood at the waiting-room doorway with a technician at her side. He rose and met them outside the door. He slipped his arm around Peyton's shoulders. "How did it go?"

She shrugged. "Okay, I guess."

He turned his attention to the young woman. He caught a glimpse of her name tag. Julie Long. "Do you know what took so long?"

"Dr. Timmons ordered an echocardiogram plus bloodwork." Julie offered a half grin. "We're extra busy today so it took longer."

What's new? Ross drew up his shoulders. "What now?"

Julie gave him a questioning look. "You're free to go. Someone will get back to you once Dr. Timmons receives the reports."

"Did everything look—"

"Sorry, Mr. Salburg." She shook her head. "I don't read the tests. You'll have to ask Peyton's physician."

He knew that, but he always hoped he might hear something hopeful. "Thanks."

He picked up Peyton's jacket from the chair he'd vacated and held it for her to slip on. "Let's go out to lunch. What do you say?"

"Can we go to Red Robin?"

He drew her to his side and gave her a one-arm hug. "Why not?"

For once, her steps bounced beside him, and the animation uplifted him. One day, she could run and play like other kids. That had been his prayer since she was diagnosed. But he'd had a similar prayer for her mother. God didn't listen.

Inside the parking structure, Ross located his van and opened the door for Peyton. When he headed for his door, he thought about Kelsey again. He'd opened the passenger door on their first real date and walked with her to the porch. *I always walk my dates to the door,* he'd told her. He'd been raised a gentleman. One day Peyton would have a young man walk her to the door. The image burned in his mind. He wanted to see her healthy and married. He wanted her to be a mother. He would be a grandfather. This time he prayed the Lord would listen.

Shame scuffled through him as he slid into the driver's seat. He knew better. The Lord didn't always say yes to prayer. He'd learned that from childhood, but a no, when talking life and death, seemed unloving. God is love. He'd read that in the Bible. So what was loving about taking his wife and maybe his daughter? How could a loving God do that?

"Dad?"

He stared at the windshield and then Peyton. "What?"

"Why are we just sitting here?"

Why? Good question. Ross slipped the key into the ignition and turned it, then backed up and headed for the exit. Before he reached it, his cell phone rang. He raised his hip and pulled it from his pocket. His pulse lurched. Kelsey.

"What's up?" He hoped he sounded casual.

"You didn't come to the MOSK meeting today."

"I'm just leaving the hospital. Peyton had—"

"Peyton? Is something wrong?" Panic filled her voice.

"Just tests her doctor ordered. Typical bloodwork and a heart echo. No results yet. I have to make an appointment with Dr. Timmons once they let me know the reports are in."

"You scared me." A stream of air filtered through the line. "I thought you'd come to the meeting today, so I wondered."

"Next week…unless something else happens."

"I hope not. The ladies are anticipating your visit. They're curious, I suppose."

"I suppose." He pictured a group of women gaping at him throughout the meeting. How could he relax and open up with that kind of pressure? Though he'd thought being part of the group might be helpful, now he began to question his enthusiasm.

"Ross?"

He yanked his head upward, her concern in her voice. "I'm here."

"You were quiet." Now she was. "I noticed Hanson is doing a concert at Joe Louis Arena."

"Hanson?" The name sounded vaguely familiar but that was it. "What kind of music does he sing?"

"They're a group. Three brothers, Zac and..." The other names escaped her. "Lucy loves them, and I thought it might be nice to take the girls to see them. It's next week, and I could pick up some tickets if you think Peyton would enjoy it."

No wonder the name only rang a small bell. "Let me ask her." He gave Peyton a look. "Would you like to go to a concert?"

"Concert?" Her eyes widened. "To see who?"

"Hanson."

A grin stole over her face. "Hanson. I love them, and I've never been to a concert."

"Would you like to? Kelsey wants to pick up four tickets."

Her mouth formed the word *four*. "We'd go with Kelsey and Lucy?"

"It might be fun." He held his breath.

She nodded. "Okay."

Air slipped from his lungs. "Great. She'd love to go. If you pick them up, I'll pay."

"It'll be my treat."

Nothing would convince her otherwise. He gave up and slipped the phone back in his pocket. "A concert will be fun, don't you think?"

Though she said yes, he heard resignation in her voice. The cords in his neck tightened and he stretched them, wishing she sounded more excited. If Kelsey hadn't come up with the idea, he would never have thought of it. He wanted to explain that to Peyton, but then he feared he would come across as a thoughtless dad. He didn't have an ounce of female awareness. He needed to concentrate on what women enjoyed. He wanted to please Peyton, but just as much, he wanted to let Kelsey know how much he cared.

Lucy and Peyton twisted in their seats to watch the Detroit scenery flash past as the People Mover stopped at stations along the path until they reached Joe Louis Arena. Ross suggested they eat in Greektown and then use the rails as a mode of travel to the concert. It made sense and shortened their walk to the arena, which is what Peyton needed.

Kelsey had kept an eye on Peyton as they made their way from the New Hellas Café to the Greektown station. Lucy charged ahead, and while Peyton made an effort to keep up with her, she soon lagged behind. When her hand went to her heart, Kelsey panicked. "Are you okay?"

Peyton dragged in a deep breath and nodded.

Ross swung around and rested his hand on his daughter's shoulder. "You can't always keep up with Lucy, Peyton. You know that. It's better to walk with us. We'll get there."

Kelsey gazed at Lucy's hurried steps, grateful that for the past year she'd led a normal life. When the last brain tumor had been removed, she'd hoped, as she always did, that Lucy would not have to undergo any more surgeries. But in the back of her mind, the nudge of worry always came. Recently, however, her fear had taken a vacation. A much-needed vacation. Grateful that Lucy was doing well, Lucy needed to be thoughtful of Peyton.

Kelsey quickened her steps and caught up with Lucy. She grasped her arm. "Hang on and stay with us."

Lucy's head tilted upward, her face screwed into a frown. "Why do I have to slow down, Mom? Everybody's excited."

"We have assigned seating. Our seats will be there. We need to stick together." She bit back what she wanted to say.

Lucy narrowed her eyes. "We have to walk slow for Peyton, don't we? Otherwise you'd be walking faster, too."

She would, but Lucy's complaint disappointed her. "Be kind, Lucy. It's not like you to not think of others. Remember when you were sick."

"I know, but that's the problem. I've been sick so much, and I'm finally better now. I don't want to be restricted anymore." Her face puckered with tears brimming her lashes.

Kelsey slipped her arm around her and pulled her to her side as they walked. "I understand, but let's try to be thoughtful, okay?"

Lucy remained silent, and though Kelsey understood, she hoped that Lucy would show kindness when they were with Peyton. The trip could be taxing on her and they still had stairs to face in the arena. She gave Lucy a squeeze and lowered her arm as she glanced over her shoulder to make sure Ross and Peyton were behind them. She slowed even more until they caught up.

"Can I at least have a treat?" Lucy's tone echoed her earlier complaint.

"You ate at the café. Are you still hungry?" She needed to give on this one or she'd never hear the end of it from Lucy.

"Just an ice cream and a drink."

Kelsey eyed Ross. "Is it okay if I buy Peyton a treat?" Though she didn't want Ross to hear Lucy's complaint, she hoped he would say yes.

"Is Lucy having something?"

She told him, and Peyton agreed that she wanted the same thing.

"This is on me then." Ross dug into his pocket, pulled out some bills and handed the money to Peyton. "Get in line now. It's long, and we'll wait here."

The girls walked off together, and Ross stood beside her, a curious look growing on his face. "Something wrong?"

Kelsey wanted to avoid the topic. She'd already warned Ross about the possible problem, and it had appeared as she had anticipated it might. "It's nothing."

"Lucy's angry."

It wasn't a question, but a statement, and Kelsey flinched. "More like frustrated. It's what I've worried about." She drew in a breath. "I talked to her about slowing down for Peyton's sake."

"Don't make a big deal out of it, or these two will never be friends."

She suspected that might be the case anyway. Lucy was too spunky for Peyton. She'd hurt Peyton's feelings without even realizing it, and she was competitive. Lucy wanted to win games. Peyton was more of a pouter, yet she wanted things her way. If Peyton would speak out and fight for herself, she would do better. Kelsey slammed her thoughts into a box. "We can only hope, Ross. Friendship grows in its time. We can't force it."

"I know, but I…"

She placed her hand on his arm. "I do, too. I'd like to see the girls become friends. It would be nice for both of them. Still I don't want us to be disappointed if that doesn't happen."

He lowered his head with a nod. With the discussion of Lucy and Peyton, the fun evening had become a downer once again. She eyed the girls. They had advanced closer to the counter. They looked cute together, Peyton with her long brown hair and Lucy's blond halo of curls. Although today the halo didn't fit her attitude.

Memories awakened in her. The first time she held Lucy in her arms something stirred inside her. Hopes and dreams spilled into her mind. But then a few years ago, things had changed and she prayed Lucy would see her teen years. Yet today, she was healthy and heading for eleven. Joy coursed through her. She prayed that those bad days were over for good.

As she studied the girls, Kelsey's attention settled on Peyton. She was an inch or more taller than Lucy, and today she noticed that Peyton's figure had begun to blossom. Lucy still looked more girlish. Seeing it made her ache for Ross. One day he'd mentioned having to face the task of explaining things to her. That was usually a mother's job, but Ross would handle it alone.

The hawkers' voices boomed in her ears. Above their heads flashed expensive souvenir booklets with photographs of the Hanson brothers, and Kelsey hoped the girls wouldn't notice the pitch. They would glance at the pictures and toss the expensive booklet into a drawer...or on the floor, which seemed to be the place Lucy liked to store things these days, including her clothes. Kelsey grinned. Maybe she was just practicing for her teen years.

"Kelsey."

Ross's voice drew her back. "Sorry. I was thinking about the girls."

"I suspected you were." He slipped his arm around her back. "I'm sorry that I brought that up again. We were having a great time, and as soon as the girls come into the conversation, something happens. I understand, but I feel the barricade rise between us. I don't want that."

"I don't want it, either, Ross. Let's be patient and give the girls a chance to get to know each other without us hovering. Maybe we're trying to do too much with them." She searched his eyes. "Do you think we should back off?"

"You have a point." A sigh rolled through him.

"Since we're on the subject of the girls, have you heard from Peyton's physician yet about her tests?"

"The receptionist called to say the tests are in, and I made an appointment. Dr. Timmons doesn't do much on the phone, and I wish he would. Then I'd know."

Those feelings weren't new to Kelsey. "Don't forget to call me when you hear."

Ross nodded and tilted his head toward the concession line. "They're getting their snacks now, so before they come back, I want to tell you that no matter what problems we're having I don't want them to affect our relationship. I told you before, but your friendship means a lot to me." He studied her face. "A lot."

Her stomach tightened. "I feel the same way."

"Then let's agree that the next date is just us."

Date. The word skipped across her heart. "Okay. Just us."

Us. She remembered the day *us* died for her. Her husband confessed his affair, and her life fell apart. Trusting was still difficult, but Ross always seemed so honest that she believed what he said. Maybe the Lord had an *us* planned for her one day again when their chaotic lives calmed down, and they could plan a future together, instead of trying to divide their days.

Chapter Eight

The doorbell's chime drew Kelsey to the door. When she opened it, Ross stood there, unsmiling. Stress etched his face.

"Hi. I hope you don't mind I dropped by without calling."

He looked desolate, and she ached for him. "No, it's fine." She stepped back, opening the door wider. "Any news on Peyton?" She reached for his jacket.

"Today." He drew up his shoulders and shrugged it off.

"Not good news." Her question wasn't needed. She knew from the look on his face. "What is it, Ross?"

He ambled into the room and plopped on the sofa. "It could be worse, but Timmons upped her blood thinner this time. If she could only get her arrhythmia under control, that would help."

"That affects her activities, I know." She sank into a chair near him. Though she wanted to be upbeat and say something positive, concern pulled at her face.

"It restricts her more than she's already restricted. I worry that the school will suggest she be homeschooled with a visiting teacher dropping in once a week. I don't want to think of that happening. I'm glad to help her with her studies, but it kills me for her. She already feels alienated, and this will just broaden the gap."

Ross pushed himself up from the sofa and paced to the window and back as if he were waiting for someone, but Kelsey guessed he was only waiting for answers for his daughter's healing.

She rose and met him in the middle of the living room, slipping her hands to his shoulders. "You know my heart is breaking for you."

He searched her eyes. "I know. You really care, and that means more than I can say. You're strong and I feel so lost sometimes."

She brushed his cheek with her palm. "Funny, because I've thought that about you."

His eyebrows arched. "One of us is confused." A faint smile touched his lips.

She let her hand drop to his and pulled him forward. "Let's have some coffee. It won't solve our problems, but maybe caffeine will stimulate our brain cells."

"Maybe." A short chuckle left him as he followed her through the dining room to the kitchen. She motioned him to sit at the table while she poured the coffee and carried it to him. "You dropped Peyton off at school?"

He nodded. "I want to keep things as normal as I can for her."

She slipped onto the chair. "And what about you? What are you doing for yourself?"

A blank look filled his eyes. "I don't know what you mean?"

"This stress is taking a toll on you, Ross. Come to MOSK Wednesday. Share these things and listen to the others. I know it won't change anything, but you said it yourself. Maybe you can learn a way to cope or hear something that will help."

A lengthy breath escaped him. "Now that I had you fight for me, sometimes I think it was a mistake. I'm not sure I can open up like I can to you. I know you and I—"

"You'll never know if you don't try."

He closed his eyes, his head nodding. "You're right. The other day I began to realize that I'm avoiding it. It kills me to know you fought a battle for me, and now I'm acting like a coward."

"Coward?" She reached across the table and grasped his hand. "Not a coward. A hero who's not looking forward to a new battle, but you will win."

"I will. Yes."

"Good. I really think you'll—"

The telephone jarred their conversation. It always did when Lucy was away from home. "Excuse me a minute." She headed for the phone across the room. She gazed at the caller ID and froze. She longed to turn and walk away, but Kelsey forced herself to pick up the headset.

"Kelsey, this is Karen. I hated to call you, but I thought I should for Lucy's sake."

Lucy's sake. Hearing from her ex-friend not only startled Kelsey, but triggered the bitter feelings she'd lugged around since Karen ran off with her husband. "What is it?"

"It's Doug. He's very ill and—"

Her words vanished in a sob. Kelsey braced herself.

"It's pancreatic cancer, Kelsey."

Pancreatic. The word squeezed against her heart. The worst. "What stage?"

"Three. It's in the lymph nodes."

The news startled her. Doug was Lucy's father. Though he'd been remiss in seeing her—more like neglectful—the fact remained. "I'm sorry, Karen." How long? The question hung on her lips but couldn't be uttered.

"I know he hasn't been a good father to Lucy. I bugged him sometimes, but you know how he is. He kept putting it off, and the longer he waited the harder it was."

Kelsey knew and didn't want to hear his excuses. She tried

to find appropriate words, but every thought that came to her was piled with anger and resentment.

"He wants to see Lucy, Kelsey."

"Now?" The word shot from her. "You're asking me to..." To what? Give a dying man his last wish. "Lucy's been through a difficult time, and—"

"I know. Doug couldn't handle it. When—"

"Couldn't handle it? Karen, you were once my friend. I was left alone to handle it. No support from Doug or you." Self-pity tore through her.

"Kelsey, would you have accepted my help?"

Shame lodged in her chest. "Probably not. You're right, but I would have appreciated a little support from Doug."

She leaned against the wall, torn with her response. "I'll talk with Lucy and see if she's up to it." The statement was moot. Lucy was up to everything. She had gained strength from fighting her own battle.

Kelsey swallowed her frustration. "Is there treatment? Surgery?"

"He has options." Karen's voice cracked. "But he's not sure he wants to go through it when the outcome is clear."

Reality pressed against her stomach, and for a moment, her mind flew back to the years she'd been in love with Doug and the good times they'd had. But he'd ruined it all with his betrayal of their marriage vows. Vows that had meant everything to her.

Kelsey lifted her gaze, startled to see Ross sitting across the great room, staring out the window. She'd forgotten. "Karen, I'll talk to Lucy and call you back. She's in school now." She glanced at her watch. Only four hours before she had to break the news to Lucy that her father was dying.

"Is she doing better now? Kelsey..." Her name had almost vanished in a whisper. "I'm so sorry. I should have asked earlier."

"You had other things on your mind." And so did she. Her

gaze settled on Ross. She'd never told him about Doug, and she wondered what he was thinking. "I have company right now, Karen. I'll call you later this evening after I talk with Lucy."

When she hung up, she stood a moment, sorry that Ross had to hear her conversation. She should have gone into her bedroom. Anywhere but to let him hear her bitterness and self-pity.

"I'm sorry, Ross. I had no idea the call would take so long."

He turned to face her, his eyes questioning. "I should have taken a walk and given you privacy."

"No. It's best you were here." She motioned for him to sit and warmed his coffee. "You've never asked, and I've never talked about my ex."

He grasped the cup and took a sip. "I've wondered, but didn't want to pry."

"I should have told you long ago. You told me about Ruthie." She had always avoided the memories. Too much pain. "Do you have time to listen?"

"I'd like to hear what happened. I assume the call was from him."

"About him. It was from his wife, Karen." She drew in a lengthy breath and told Ross about Doug and Karen's betrayal. She didn't delve into details. Not today.

"Your best friend?" He looked dazed. "And you never suspected?"

"Gullible. Stupid. Blind." Her chest tightened with the memory of the hurt and mortification she dealt with when she found out.

"Deceived by your two best friends." He shook his head. "I can't even imagine."

Neither could Kelsey. "I should have caught on." She thought back to clues she'd brushed away, slips of the tongue she'd ignored.

"How did you find out?"

The day stabbed her. "Her husband figured it out and called me."

Ross's eyes widened as he drew back. "He called you. That must have been horrible."

"I still didn't believe it. I thought he was mixed up. Had the wrong person. You know. I did everything to convince him he was wrong until he said enough things that I had to face the truth."

Ross leaned forward and grasped her hand.

"You know what Doug said when I confronted him?"

"I can't imagine."

"He said, 'I never wanted you to know.'" Despite the painful memory, she chuckled at the absurdity. "How do you respond to that? Naturally, he didn't want me to know."

Ross shook his head, amazement on his face. "I'm glad you can laugh about it now."

"I've risen above it. Moved on." Had she really? "But the phone call dredged up a lot of emotion."

"Why did she call?"

Gooseflesh rose up her arm. "Doug has pancreatic cancer. He's in stage three."

He lowered his head. "Horrible."

"It is…especially for Lucy." The thought bolted through her, and she rose on trembling legs. "I have to tell her when she gets home, and I don't know how she'll take it."

"It's her dad. I suppose she'll—"

"He's her father pretty much in name only. He hasn't been around. An occasional call and, when he remembers, a gift for Christmas or her birthday."

A frown deepened on his face.

"But to be fair, I didn't push it. I didn't want to face them, so their absence was better for me than their presence." What she'd said to Karen jogged her mind. *I was left alone to handle it. No support from Doug or you.* It reeked of self-pity.

Ross drew her into his arms. "What you did seems natural to me. Don't fault yourself. A father of any worth would insist on being with his daughter. You couldn't stop him if you wanted to."

Though he was right, Kelsey questioned her reaction, in retrospect. "Maybe a little urging would have gotten some action. Lucy would have known her father better than she does now."

He pressed his cheek to hers. "It's so hard to do the right thing when you're wounded, and you were, Kelsey."

He kissed her cheek and drew her closer. She felt her heart beating against his chest, his strong arms protecting her.

"I wish I could be there with you when you talk to Lucy, but I know I can't." He tilted her chin and looked into her eyes. "I want to be here for you, Kelsey, in any way I can. Just ask."

Tears bubbled to the surface and rested on her lashes. His kindness overwhelmed her. She'd never experienced that kind of caring, and all her questions about their fated relationship seemed pointless now, and they vanished with his touch. "Thank you. Really. But talking to Lucy is something I have to do alone."

"I know it is."

She stood in his arms, dreading the moment that Lucy came home and dreading Ross leaving. When she faced her singleness, she often wondered what the future had in store for her—what God had in store for her—and she'd been taunted by the Bible verse that rang in her head. *Two are better than one.* She had become a one, but today the words held a different meaning. *If one falls down, his friend can help him up.* She clung to Ross's muscular frame, knowing that she wouldn't fall with him at her side.

Thank You, Lord.

* * *

Ross stood in the doorway of the MOSK meeting, gathering courage. Kelsey had been correct. He needed to be here, so he'd pushed away the negative talk in his head and forced himself to attend. When he came through the door, he faced a group of women. No other men were in attendance—he'd hoped that maybe one other brave soul had decided to take advantage of the organization's new policy...to open the group to male members on a trial basis.

The word trial irked him, but he had to be grateful they were willing to try, and he had to admit, he could have easily passed up the offer himself without Kelsey's encouragement. She thought he was strong. He wasn't. His strength came from prayer and common sense. Men were expected to handle things.

Kelsey smiled and patted the seat next to her.

He wandered to her side, curious about her discussion with Lucy. She hadn't called, and he decided to give her time to deal with the difficult situation that he'd witnessed. He settled into the chair beside her and studied her face before asking. "How's Lucy?"

"She's okay. It was hard to tell her. She cried a little. I knew she would. Lucy has a soft, forgiving heart. Lucy talked about her dad's neglectful ways, but always with words of forgiveness. She offered reasons. He traveled so much and he lived quite a long distance away. I let her talk without comment. I knew not to put down her dad, even though I felt so much bitterness."

"Good for you. That's not easy."

Kelsey eyed her watch. "Time to start." She rose and faced the women. "Today I'd like to introduce you to a good friend of mine."

Ross's chest ached, holding back his anxiety. The muscles in his neck had become iron rods, and though he tried to relieve the tension, he couldn't do it without making it obvious. "This is Ross Salburg, and he'll be joining us based on our vote that we'll open our meetings to men and see how it goes."

Ross wanted to escape, but he grasped the chair seat and forced himself to smile and give the women a wave.

Diane Dodge raised her hand. "Welcome, Ross. I'm so glad you've finally made it. Now that you've appeared, I can get my husband to come. He's been waiting."

Ross chuckled. "So he didn't want to be the first guy to attend?"

"Right. I told him he was cowardly." She tittered. "He's not, but I thought the comment would motivate him. Obviously it didn't."

Some women chuckled.

"We'll look forward to him being with us next week, Diane. Tell him he's welcome."

Kelsey waved her finger from one side of the room to the other. "So let's get in our circle and begin."

Chairs scraped as the women shifted into a circle and once everyone was settled, Kelsey opened the meeting. "Since you shared the news about your husband, Diane, tell us how everything else is going."

She began, followed by the next woman. Ross's throat ached, holding back emotions he hadn't allowed to surface when tears were shed as one mother spoke of her son's relapse. Each woman offered a word of encouragement, and the thoughts and concerns circled the room. The circle narrowed to him, and his hands trembled as he folded them in his lap, trying to hang on to his composure.

Kelsey motioned for him to begin, and he cleared his throat, hoping his voice would sound firm and in control. "As you already know, I'm Ross. My daughter, Peyton, who just turned twelve, has cardiomyopathy."

A gasp sizzled around the room. Ross dug his nails into the base of the chair. He knew what they were thinking, and he didn't want to hear their thoughts or face them. He gathered his wits. "Peyton has done quite well. I spotted the symptoms, because my wife…" He didn't want to go there. Fifteen women stared at him, their faces filled with question. "Because my wife had died from cardiomyopathy a few years earlier."

Shock registered on their faces, and this time their oohs reached him. They were empathizing. He knew that, but he'd never allowed people to share his grief—not until Kelsey came along. He glanced at her and saw her caring expression. He could see that she wanted to touch him, to give him a pat of confidence, but it was impossible in the room full of women.

Ross decided to barrel along. He told them about her symptoms, her tests and now his sadness at having to up her meds. "She has a difficult time with other kids. You know how they are. She misses school when she's not doing well, and she feels out of it. Instead of going back to classes and joining in, she pulls away."

"And that causes the others to pull away."

He guessed that the comment came from the woman who'd introduced herself as Shirley. He nodded. "So that's where I'm at now. Praying that her arrhythmia lessens, and we can decrease the coumadin."

"I'll add that to my prayer list," Shirley said, compassion filling her face. "I'll also pray for her ability to make friends."

"Thanks, Shirley."

A few other women joined in with comments on prayer, and Ross's spirit lifted. He'd shared his story, and he received offers for prayer. He could do this, and maybe next time, he wouldn't be so tense. He had so much more he could tell them, and he needed answers.

Chairs were shifted back and a short meeting followed. Women offered new ideas for sharing, films they'd seen, programs at hospitals for parents. It ended more quickly than he'd expected. He hung around, wanting to know more about Kelsey's plans with Lucy, and when the last woman left the room, he rose from the chair. "What are you planning to do now that Lucy knows? Does she want to see him?"

Kelsey leaned her hip against the desk. "Yes, but I knew she would."

"So what will you do?"

"He lives in Grand Rapids. I'll take her there on Saturday, make sure she's inside and then find something to do while they visit. They can call me on my cell phone when she's ready to be picked up."

"Saturday." He tossed the idea around in his head. "Do you want company?"

"Company?" She eyed him and her eyes brightened. "You're willing to come along?"

"Very willing. I'll see if I can get a sitter for Peyton." His comment fluttered across her face.

"You could bring her if you want."

"I could." He pictured the sober occasion, but Peyton had never been to Grand Rapids that he could remember and bringing her might be a good distraction for Lucy.

"It's up to you, but I'd love your company."

Something registered in her eyes that he didn't comprehend. Maybe she had the same thoughts. Peyton would not only be a distraction, but the sad occasion might offer Peyton a chance to show sympathy and heighten their friendship.

A deep sigh rolled from Kelsey. "This will be hard for me."

"I'm sure it will." He couldn't imagine Ruthie having an affair. Trust, confidence, everything defiled by lust and betrayal.

Kelsey dragged her fingers through her hair, forcing her part to vanish for a moment. "I've only seen Karen a couple of times since I learned about the affair and that was always from a distance. I dealt with Doug."

"I'll be with you. I can't work wonders, but maybe having a friend there will help."

"It will, and I can't thank you enough."

He walked to her side, longing to hold her in his arms. The almost-kiss still hung in his memory, waiting to happen. He'd monitored his emotions so long now he feared taking the step. He gazed at her lips, her soft cheeks and her long, silken hair. His pulse escalated. He looked around the empty room but stopped himself. This wasn't the right time. Another opportunity would come, and hopefully her sitter wouldn't turn on the porch light next time.

Chapter Nine

Kelsey steered Lucy through the doorway while Ross waited on the porch. He'd worn a suede jacket and beneath it, a pull-over in beige and camel, the same color as the suede. He looked so good to her—a stalwart, caring friend—who put her needs first, first after Peyton. Nearing his minivan, she saw it was empty.

"Where's Peyton?"

He glanced at Lucy and closed the distance between them. "The more I thought about it, the more I didn't like the idea. Peyton would be bored with the waiting, and Mrs. Withers was available. It made more sense." He slipped his hand into hers and gave it a squeeze. "And we can use the alone time."

Grateful, she pressed his hand to affirm his decision. Her emotions had been tied in knots since she'd made plans for the trip, and she'd been concerned about Peyton's presence, but telling Ross she wasn't welcome didn't seem right. He'd made a good choice.

Though Lucy sat in the back seat, a novel in her hand, Kelsey could see she was apprehensive, not only facing her father after so long, but knowing he was very ill. Kelsey gri-maced at her decision to hold back the truth from her daughter. She didn't have it in her heart to tell Lucy that her father was dying. It seemed like too much at one time.

Now she wondered how Doug would react to seeing Lucy. She'd grown up a little—she was more a young lady than a child. Ten was that in-between age when young girls floundered with one foot in childhood and another stretching for adulthood. They wanted to be treated as adults, having their own freedom and independence, while clinging to the security and easy life of their youth. And then came attitude. Sometimes Lucy rolled her eyes as if mothers were the most stupid people in the world. At times, Kelsey believed it.

"You're thoughtful."

Her stomach lurched. "Thinking." She felt empty. "So many memories and concerns."

"I can't even imagine." He snapped on the radio and turned down the volume. "You don't have to talk now. I know you have a lot to think about." He glanced into the rearview mirror. "Lucy's sleeping, I think."

She turned around and saw her daughter's eyes closed, the book resting on the seat beside her. "I don't think she slept well." She stretched her neck to relieve the tension. "Neither did I."

He slipped his hand to hers. "Take a nap, too. You need a clear mind for this."

The warmth traveled to her heart. "I do." She closed her eyes and relaxed to the lilt of the music and the rhythm of the highway.

"Kelsey, I think we're close."

She opened her eyes, startled that she'd fallen asleep. Ross's hand rested on her arm. She scooted up in the seat and tried to wrap her mind around where she was and why. The answer hit her, and her stomach knotted. Eyeing the surroundings, she got her bearings. "I've only been here a couple of times. At first, Doug came to Clawson." A building came into sight that she recognized. "Turn right up here."

Ross followed her directions and as they rolled down Doug's street, she leaned over her seat and tapped Lucy. "Wake up, sleepyhead."

Lucy's eyes flew open, and she looked around, her dazed eyes widening. "Are we there already?"

"Almost."

She straightened in the seat and ran her hand over her hair. "Mom, do you have a comb?"

Kelsey grinned and dug into her purse. "Here you go." She handed her the comb and Lucy ran it through her curls. She handed it back, mumbling a thanks.

"We should have brought him something." Kelsey looked at Ross for validation. "Lucy, you should take a gift for your dad since he's ill. Flowers or candy. Maybe a magazine. Anything."

Hindered by the seat belt, Lucy scooted as close as she could get. "Mom, aren't flowers for girls?"

Kelsey eyed Ross. "What do you say?"

"Some men like flowers, but all men like candy."

"See, Mom. Let's buy him a box of chocolates."

Kelsey stretched her mind and recalled a drugstore not far away. She gave Ross directions and soon they were back where they'd started. When they pulled in front of Doug's house, she drew in a calming breath. "I'll walk you to the door, Lucy, but I'm not going to stay." She dug into her purse and pulled out a slip of paper. "Here's my cell-phone number in case you've forgotten it, and—"

"Mom." She rolled her eyes. "I know your number."

"Okay." She dropped the scrap into her purse. "I hope that's all right."

Lucy shrugged. "I'd rather you were there, too."

Air emptied from Kelsey's lungs. "I know, but it's better for you and your dad to spend time together without me there. I'd just be in the way. You know that your dad and I—"

"But he's sick now."

Guilt shriveled her argument. "Ross drove us here, because he knew we were upset. I don't want to leave him alone while—"

"Kelsey, don't worry—"

She flashed him a scowl. "You'd be waiting a long time alone, Ross. I can't do that to you."

"It's okay." Lucy's voice slid into the conversation. "I understand."

Relief swilled over her cowardice. Where was her spunk? She'd never hurt Doug or Karen. They'd hurt her, and why couldn't she let it die? The word stabbed her. *Die.* Doug. She peered at the house and noticed the front door open.

"They've seen us." She faced Lucy. "Ready?"

She nodded and unlatched her seat belt. As she did, an unexpected prayer slipped into Kelsey's thoughts. A prayer for her attitude and a prayer for Lucy's day. God would protect her.

Ross opened his door, and she grasped his arm. "Not this time."

He seemed to understand and closed the door.

She clutched the door handle and stepped out, hoping her legs would hold her steady. Lucy waited on the sidewalk, clutching the box of chocolates. She looked too young to bear this difficult visit alone, but Kelsey sensed it would be for the best. Her scars were still raw after so many years, and she feared that hiding her bitterness would be impossible. This wasn't a time for resentment, but compassion—and she didn't have it.

Ahead she saw Karen standing behind the storm door. When they were friends, she would have waved and smiled, but today her arm clung to her side, her lips straight as a razor and just as sharp.

Karen pushed open the door. "Lucy." She crouched and gave her a hug. "Your daddy is so anxious to see you."

Lucy lost her voice and only gave a nod, staring ahead as

if she wanted to get inside and see her father. Karen stood back and waved her in. "It's good to see you, Kelsey. You look well."

"Thank you." She took a step back.

"Aren't you coming in?"

"No. This should be time for Lucy and her father." She motioned to the car. "I have a friend who drove us here."

Karen's head jerked toward the minivan, and she squinted. "That was nice of him."

"He's a wonderful man. Very thoughtful and caring." She wanted to add *trustworthy* to the list, but she stopped herself.

"I'm glad for you." Karen's eyes searched hers. "I really am."

"When Lucy's ready to leave, would you let her call my cell phone?" She should have said thank you or acknowledged her *glad-for-you* comment, but the words wouldn't come. Animosity proved to be a horrible emotion, and letting it go hadn't happened.

"She'll have lunch with us, if that's okay."

Kelsey took another step back. "It's fine. Just have her call when she's about ready and we'll come back to pick her up." She turned and took a step.

"Kelsey."

She spun around.

"Thanks for bringing her today. It means a lot to Doug."

Deep in her core, she seethed with the violence of a volcano ready to erupt. The burning smoke filled her chest and scorched her throat, waiting to spew her frustration into Karen's face, but she lifted her eyes to Ross, and did what she had to do. Keep the festering fire inside. As she strode away, she sent up a prayer of thanks that God had given her a friend like him, and she prayed for her heart's healing. She'd licked her wounds long enough.

"How was it?" Ross opened the passenger door and she slid inside.

"Rough, and I'm ashamed of myself."

His brows lifted. "What did you say?"

As he pulled away, she told him what she'd done and the thoughts she'd been able to squelch. "Ripping her with my feelings would have accomplished nothing. Do you know what I did?"

He shook his head.

"I looked at you, and thanked God for the gift."

He dropped one hand from the steering wheel and covered hers. "I'm happy you feel that way. Sometimes I question the wisdom of our relationship. I know people have said things to you, and I've heard a few comments myself. Nothing terrible, but asking how we manage with two sick children. I don't like to think of it that way, but their words make it a reality."

She lifted her shoulders. "I'm not crazy about reality, either. And as far as we are concerned, so far so good."

He gave her hand a pat and grasped the steering wheel. "What should we do while we wait? How about lunch?"

She eyed her watch. "It's a little early yet. Let's check out the art museum. I hear it's terrific." And hopefully it would give her time to cool down.

"Sounds good. We can find a place to have lunch downtown."

"What is it with men and thoughts of food?" She smiled and it felt good.

He grinned back and patted his trim belly. "Food's good, but being with you is better."

Sometimes she thought her life had become too good to be true. And that worried her.

"It is terrific. You were right." Ross stood near the reflecting pool at Rosa Park Circle, admiring the cantilevered concrete portico that thrust outward from the museum. "An amazing sight. Being a contractor, all I can say is one word. *Powerful.*"

"It is. I know someone who comes here and mentioned it. I can use a relaxing distraction."

"Thinking of Lucy, aren't you?" He didn't need to hear her response. Kelsey had been quiet since they'd left Doug's house.

She nodded. "But this is nice. The museum couldn't have a nicer setting than this park."

He wrapped his arm around her shoulders. "If it was warmer, we could sit outside and enjoy the view."

She leaned into him with a chuckle. "So let's check it out." She motioned to the museum.

He lowered his arm and grasped her hand, weaving his fingers through hers. When the girls were around, he tried to be more discreet and sometimes it killed him. Today they had time alone, but, as always, Lucy and Peyton hung in their minds.

They wandered inside, and he stopped again to admire another reflecting pool glinting in the winter sun. April was on their doorstep, and he longed for those warmer days when they could sit in the park and enjoy a picnic or a bike ride with the girls. His chest constricted. Would Peyton be able to ride a bike? He could only pray and wait for the blessing.

"Nice." Kelsey motioned to the wide hallways with shining oak flooring and white walls that set off the masterpieces of art.

He sensed her distraction, and when he spotted a bench, he motioned for them to sit. She followed his suggestion and sank onto the concrete. He joined her, wishing he had words to make things better. "Lucy will do okay, and I'm sure her dad is thrilled to see her. If he's facing death, Kelsey, maybe he'll want to make up for the years of negligence."

"Can anyone make up for those years, Ross?" She shook her head in answer to her own question.

He couldn't blame her, but he wished he understood more fully. "You've been single a long time now, Kelsey. You're a kind, loving person, and it doesn't suit you to carry the anger so long." From her expression, he'd struck a nerve.

"Maybe I'm angry at myself for not wanting to face the affair. I always explained it away."

Emotions caught Ross off guard. The tender feeling filled him. "How long did it go on before you found out?"

"A year or more."

He shook his head, startled at how long she'd been deceived, but it showed how trusting Kelsey had been. That's what a marriage should be.

"Doug traveled for his job, and now that I look back, I have no idea when he was really on a business trip or somewhere with Karen. Sometimes when he was going out of town, I'd try to make plans with her. You know, a girls' night out. Once in a while, we'd go to a movie or out to dinner, but more and more she had excuses. She had an out-of-town wedding or a sick aunt or something. It was easy to think coincidence."

"I suppose you can be grateful they went out of town. No gossip that way."

Her face twisted with emotion. "He wasn't that bright. Once in a while someone would mention seeing him with Karen. When I asked, he'd make a joke about how good it was that I was trusting." She dragged in a breath. "I tossed it off, and then I'd ask. He'd make up some excuse. They happened to be in the same restaurant and decided to sit together."

"It happens." No matter what he said, it sounded trivial. "A husband and wife should be trusting. If they're not, the marriage isn't healthy. Yours was."

"One-sided." He watched a kaleidoscope of emotion sweep over her eyes.

"Ross, I know you're right. Why can't I let it go? I could have at least walked inside and showed some compassion. The Bible says to love our enemies. I've failed."

"But you're sorry for it, and God forgives you."

She lifted her gaze to his. "Then why can't I forgive?"

Forgiveness always seemed like such an ordeal. He'd blamed God for Ruthie's death and Peyton's struggle with the same disease, and yet he'd faced the reality that God allowed things to happen for reasons that he would never know. He trusted the Lord, and that's what she needed to do. "You'll never forget what they did, Kelsey." He slipped his arm around her back. "But you can forgive."

She scanned the surroundings in silence until she finally turned to face him. "I'll work on it, Ross. That's all I can promise."

He drew her closer to his side. "That's all I want to hear." He glanced at his watch, surprised at the time. "We'd better head for lunch, or Lucy will call and we won't have eaten." He rose and took her hand. But from her expression, lunch was the last thing on her mind.

Kelsey stood back from the door as Lucy came out carrying a large grocery bag. Trying to be subtle, she glanced inside only to catch a glimpse of something in a shade of pastel turquoise. Gifts. Her stomach knotted. She slipped her arm around Lucy's shoulders, feeling protective, but her ire had subsided when she looked at Karen's haggard face. It looked different than it had when she'd dropped Lucy there earlier. "I'll pray for you, Karen."

Karen's head bolted upward, anxiety written on her face. "Thanks, but..." As her words dragged to a halt, gratefulness filled her face. "It's nice to hear you say that."

She'd surprised herself, but she would pray. Death and divorce were similar but different. Which was worse? No answer came, but the finality of death was a permanent emptiness.

Karen leaned down and hugged Lucy. "Your visit meant a lot to us, sweetie. I know your dad is grateful that your mom brought you for a visit." She lifted her head and faced Kelsey. "Hospice has been a great help. At least, he can be home."

Hospice. The word dug into her heart. "You think it will be…" She couldn't say anything in front of Lucy. She gazed at Karen, wondering if she and Doug had told her the truth.

"Yes. He's opted out of chemo or radiation. Quality of life is more important now."

Karen's bravery wriggled into Kelsey's chest and filled the gash. "Quality of life is best."

She nodded.

They faced each other a few moments, nothing spoken, but so much said.

Lucy tugged her arm, and she stepped back. "We'll be going, Karen. I know you'll keep us posted."

"I will." She gave a nod, along with a lingering look at Lucy. "We love you."

"Love you, too," she said, then turned and started down the porch steps.

Kelsey's knees felt weak as she trudged back to the minivan. Once inside she caught her breath. Ross gave a brief turn of his head, but didn't ask and she was relieved. She looked over the seat at Lucy. "What's in the bag?"

"Presents."

"Looks like a lot of presents."

She nodded, but without a smile.

"Dad said he was sorry he missed Christmas last year, and he gave me birthday presents for this year." She dug into the sack and then looked up. "Want to see?"

Kelsey nodded, and as Lucy pulled out the items, Ross rolled onto the highway. She'd forgotten that Doug hadn't sent gifts for Christmas. It was so like him to forget special occasions that she'd given up expecting anything. Now he wanted to be a father.

She stifled her resentment. If she were dying, Kelsey suspected she would do the same thing, try to resolve mistakes, lavish love on those important in her life and make amends for the hurts she'd caused. Ross's words filled her mind. She'd never forget, but she could forgive. Her emotions vacillated between compassion and animosity.

Lucy delved into the bag and pulled out a turquoise outfit, a print skirt and a top to match—even the right size. "And he gave me Chinese checkers." She grinned. "It's so much fun. Daddy played it with me. Have you played it, Mom?"

"A long time ago." Clothes, games. Kelsey wondered if she'd finally come to the end.

"And puzzles." She brought out two jigsaw puzzles.

She almost rolled her eyes. Doug knew she loved them, even as a toddler. He'd certainly worked to impress his daughter.

"And there's more." Lucy dug into the grocery sack again, tugging out another blouse, this one with coral trim, and then she lifted out a picture frame.

Kelsey swallowed the rising emotion as Lucy put it in her hand. Tears slipped into her eyes, and she looked away before Lucy saw them.

Brushing her hands across the dampness, she looked down at the photograph of Lucy and Doug, cheeks together, smiling. It appeared to be an older photograph—maybe two years earlier—when Lucy had visited him. Though the picture rent her heart, a familiar stab of resentment pierced her. Sarcasm clung to her tongue until she was able to consume it and respond. "It's a nice photograph, Lucy." She lowered the frame into Lucy's hands.

"Daddy said to put it on my nightstand."

Her father's suggestion grated her, but she turned her thoughts around, trying to hear Ross's voice. Forgiveness. *Lord, I'm such a sinner.* Calm waved past her like a breeze. "That way you'll see your father every morning when you wake up."

Lucy nodded, a troubled look growing on her face. "Mom."

Kelsey gazed at her. "They're nice gifts. I like them."

She slipped the photograph back into the paper bag. "Can I ask you a question?"

The sound of her voice aroused her concern. She didn't want to answer a question, but seeing Lucy's face, she had to. "Okay."

"Why didn't you go inside and see Daddy?"

Her heart skipped a beat. "I wanted you and your father to have this special time together."

"But he talked about you."

Her pulse heightened. "What do you mean?" Weight fell on her shoulders.

"He asked me if you were doing okay, and was your job real good." Her eyes searched Kelsey's. "Was it okay I told him you were fine and you had lots of work?"

"That was fine. You should always be honest."

"Oh, and I forgot. He gave me something to give you."

She delved back into the bottom of the sack and pulled out an envelope. "Maybe it's a letter." Lucy handed it to her. "Read it."

It was the last thing she wanted to do, but how could she explain that to her eager daughter? She pulled open the tab and drew out the note. When she unfolded it, a check had been tucked inside. She gazed at the amount and cringed as she scanned the message. Her chest compressed against her lungs, and she fought for breath.

"It's long, Lucy. I'll read it later. Okay?"

Lucy shrugged.

Doug's guilt for his neglect seemed obvious by the size of the check. But money wasn't the issue now, although it had been. Giving love and attention to Lucy was vital. Yet if he had shown her all of that, Kelsey would have felt she and Doug were competing for Lucy's attention.

"You should have talked with him."

Lucy's admonition startled her, and her heart softened. "Would that make you happy?"

She nodded. "He's sick, and I don't understand. He's sad, but he tried to look happy."

"Lucy, he was happy to see you, but it's difficult when an adult is sick. It means he can't work, and he can't do the things he wants to do."

Her eyes searched Kelsey's. "Will he get better?" She tilted her head, determination growing on her face.

Tension twisted through her, and Kelsey rumpled the envelope in her hand. Lucy wanted the truth. "I don't know. He's very sick and the doctors don't have much they can do."

Her face pinched with thought. "But he'll go to heaven." She tilted her head again. "Right?"

Panic set in, and Kelsey eyed Ross. He glanced her way, letting her know she had to make the decision on how to answer. The word *forgiveness* struck her again. God forgives sin when the person atones. She had no idea if Doug was sorry for what he did, but she looked at Lucy's distressed face and the answer came.

"Your dad loves you, Lucy, and when we were married, he loved Jesus. We know that when we believe in Jesus as God's Son and love him—"

"We'll go to heaven." Relief filled her face.

Kelsey wanted to reach across the seat and draw Lucy into her arms. "That's right. It's God's promise."

"Good." Lucy's shoulders relaxed, and she gazed at the bag beside her. "But I hope he doesn't die."

"So do I."

And she did, for Lucy's sake. Kelsey longed to curl up in bed and weep. Instead she closed her eyes and prayed.

Chapter Ten

Kelsey eyed the caller ID and grabbed the headset. "Audrey, what a surprise." She held her breath, fearing another problem.

"I know it's been a while." A hint of guilt edged into her sister's voice. "How's Lucy?"

"Pretty good. She's been tumor-free for over a year. That's a great victory for us." Audrey called so rarely, concern settled in her mind. "How are the kids? Mom and Dad? Everyone okay?"

"We're all well. Mom and Dad are busy, as always."

"Wonderful." Kelsey gripped the phone, the obvious question nudging her. "So what's up?"

"Jeff has business in Detroit near the end of May, and I thought I'd come with him so we could visit."

She knew she should be happy, but Kelsey had so much going on in her life—work, Lucy and now Ross. Common sense prodded her. "That would be great. Lucy and I would love to see you."

"Great." Her voice came to a dead stop.

Kelsey looked for a reason. Then it struck her. "Would you and Dave like to stay here? I have the extra room."

"That would be wonderful...if you don't mind."

Mind. She drew up her shoulders, knowing what she had to say. "It'll be more convenient for everyone, don't you think?" She'd walked around her question without lying.

"It would. Thanks. Isn't Lucy's birthday around that time?"

Kelsey cringed. "It's May 20."

"We should be there then, so we'll do something special to celebrate. Would Lucy like that?"

"Lucy would, I'm sure." Her own plans ricocheted. She'd wanted to do something with Ross and Peyton.

"I'll call you with a firm date, and thanks again. I'm looking forward to seeing you both."

"That sounds fine, Audrey. We can make better plans when you call."

The conversation died away, and when she hung up, she sank into a chair. Ross had been tied up with Peyton and his work, and they'd only been talking on the phone recently, except for one day when he dropped by for a minute. Peyton's doctor's visits and consultations had cut into their time to the point that their relationship, which had been blossoming into something deeper, seemed to be shriveling like a plant for lack of water and sunshine.

The almost-kiss crept into her mind so often. His lips had brushed hers before jerking away with the porch light's glare, and though she still had no certainty where their friendship would go, hope lingered in her mind. They were compatible. They had fun and laughed sometimes when they weren't concerned about the girls. Ross's gentle nature, his caring heart, had touched her far beyond her dreams. She'd expected to spend her life alone, fearing another romantic encounter that led to deceit, but when Ross appeared in her life—at a wedding no less—her old expectation slipped further back in her mind.

She lowered her head as Doug filtered into her thoughts. Since she'd read his letter, flashes of their marriage came to mind on occasion, a few special moments surprising her. Doug's joy when Lucy was born. Their first home. A trip to London. She would never love him again. That was impossible, but he wasn't the monster she'd created in her mind. He'd sinned and had broken his oath to God and to her. But who was she to weigh one sin over another? If the Lord could forgive Doug, why couldn't she?

She rose, pulled a mug from the cabinet and turned on the burner to heat water for tea. While waiting, she wandered into the living room and pulled open the small antique secretary desk she rarely used. She drew out the letter and held it in her hand, her throat knotting with the memory of Doug's words. Sinking into a chair, Kelsey unfolded the paper again.

> *Dear Kelsey,*
> *What can I say to you that will make up for what I've done? I betrayed you and hurt you, and I'm ashamed. You need to understand that I love Karen, and I have been faithful to her, but I owed you the same. My cheating had nothing to do with you. You always were a wonderful wife and a tremendous mother. I allowed temptation to win out over good sense. Karen has never forgiven herself, either, and we both wished we'd met years earlier so that the harm we caused would never have happened.*
>
> *But just as important, I've let my guilt turn me into a rotten father who shied away from his precious little daughter, who needed his support. You've handled her illness with bravery and strength, which I admire more than I can say. I know forgetting what I did is impossible, but I hope one day you can find it in your heart to forgive my unfaithfulness. I pray the Lord has. He's heard my pleas.*

Tears filled Kelsey's eyes and dripped onto the paper.

*I hope you will accept the check in the spirit in which
I wrote it. I want to do something for Lucy and I don't
know how to make up for my lack of presence in her
life. Money won't cover that, but maybe you can find
something she'd like, something special that would
make her remember me with love.*

A sob rent Kelsey's throat. She dropped the letter into her
lap and covered her face with her hands, allowing the hot
tears to burn away her hatred.

When the kettle whistled, she wiped the tears from her
eyes and returned the letter to the small desk. One day she
would toss it away, but not now. The kettle persisted, and she
returned to the kitchen. When her tea was ready, she wandered back to the living room, settled into the chair and rested
her head against the cushion, thinking of Lucy's recent visit
with Doug.

The evening they'd arrived home from Grand Rapids after
Ross left, she read the note and then shared what she could
with Lucy. Doug's words left her flailing with emotions that
lashed one way and then another, but in time, she'd calmed
and tried to make sense of it all.

Despite Doug's exit from her life, she'd been blessed. Her
good job, her friends and Lucy's improved health reminded
her that life was still good. And now Ross.

She lifted the mug and took a sip. It washed down her
throat, warming her, yet an icy thought prevailed. Doug's
letter made his death so real that she trembled.

Things happened without warning. Accidents, death, even
falling in love. She took another sip of tea to soothe her emptiness. She missed Ross. Peyton's illness often came between
them, and she understood, but it didn't alleviate the lonely
feeling. And sometimes she wondered if Lexie was right

when she said two people with sick children shouldn't fall in love.

But that's what she'd been doing.

Ross's concern rose as he eyed Dr. Timmons's face, his lips pressed together with a faint frown on his face. He shifted in his chair and studied Peyton's file.

Trying to contain himself, Ross clasped his hands in his lap, using the pressure to steady them.

"I don't want you to get excited." Dr. Timmons looked over the top of his glasses, his gaze shifting from Peyton to Ross.

"What is it?" Panic surged in Ross's voice.

"Nothing's wrong." Timmons rose and slipped two x-rays into the lighted slots. "This was Peyton's X-ray from six months ago." He pointed to the electrocardiogram. "You can see the size of her heart here. Now look at this x-ray."

Rigid with worry, Ross squinted, not sure what to look for. His pulse rose, searching for something different, something that would show more growth or a flaw. Then Dr. Timmons's words flashed into his mind. *I don't want you to get excited.* What did he mean by that? He searched the physician's face.

"I don't see any difference."

"That's correct. For the past year, Peyton's heart has remained stable. No enlargement at all. Her heart echo shows that her heart is working the same. Same size. Same shape. That's excellent."

Air shot from Ross's lungs. "Then that means she's doing well."

"That part of her heart is. Yes." He returned to the desk and shuffled through the file. "The greatest problem lies in the electrical system of her heart. Her arrhythmia." He lifted his gaze to Ross before looking at Peyton. "Peyton, that's why you take the blood thinner and medication for irregular heart rhythm."

"I know, and that's what restricts me." Her expression showed her unhappiness.

"It does. You have to be careful playing so as not to get cut or bruised badly and the other medication makes you short of breath, tired and feel weak sometimes."

She nodded. "I hate it."

Ross flinched at her comment and captured her attention. "Peyton, the medicine keeps you from serious problems. You've been able to go to school—yes, with restrictions— but you can go, and when you take naps and rest, you can do lots of things." He wanted to tell her she was alive, but he couldn't do that. He felt desperate and looked at Dr. Timmons for help.

"And this is why I told you not to get too excited. Recently, a new medication has been approved that may work better on Peyton. It has been doing a good job of controlling arrhythmia for some patients. Once we can stabilize your heart rhythm, we may be able to take you off coumadin."

"Really?" Peyton's eyes widened, and she clutched her hands to her chest. "Can I take that instead of what I do now?"

"I want to study this a little more before we change, and you know…" He leaned closer and looked her in the eyes. "This doesn't mean you'll be well right away. It will take time, but we could see an improvement in a few months. That would be my hope."

"It's mine, too, doctor." Ross drew in a breath, excited yet apprehensive about what he heard. He knew from other medications that they sometimes had side effects that might not work with Peyton. It was in God's hands. "So what do we do now?"

"Follow the same procedures you've been following, and I'll get back to you when I make a decision. I'll consult with a couple specialists and that will help me weigh the pros and cons for Peyton."

Ross slipped his arm around Peyton's shoulders. "What do you think?"

"I guess we have to wait and see."

Her excitement had died down with the doctor's hesitation, and Ross hoped that as they talked she would see the big picture. Everything took time, but it could be worth it.

The doctor rose. "I'll see you at her next appointment, if not before. I'll give you a call."

"I'll be waiting, Dr. Timmons."

The specialist walked to the door and opened it. "Hopefully I'll have good news for you, Peyton."

Ross rose and Peyton followed. They headed to the checkout desk in silence and then strode to the car. His mind reeled with the news. In all the excitement about the medication, he'd forgotten the other wonderful news. Peyton's heart had shown no changes for months. His feet danced to the minivan.

Once they were settled inside, his mind ticked with an idea. "School's out now so you don't have to go back. I'm sure that makes you happy."

She grinned. "It does, but I'd be happier if I knew I could have the new medication now."

"Peyton, sometimes in life, we have to wait. But, you know what? Waiting gives you something to look forward to." He patted her hand. "I believe that God's going to bless us this time."

"You mean He'll help Dr. Timmons say yes?"

"Something like that. But if not, then something better will happen. And don't forget what he said about your heart."

"It's the same as it was." She shook her head.

He pulled up his shoulders. "I think we should celebrate." She gave him a questioning look.

"It's Friday night, and how about if I call Kelsey and see if they'd like to join us. We can do something fun." Her expression didn't flicker, but he knew she was thinking.

"Like what?"

"I don't know." His mind emptied. "Let me call Kelsey, and see what she thinks."

Peyton didn't respond, but she didn't say no. That was a major victory.

He hit Kelsey's number and was disappointed when she didn't answer. Instead, he checked his contact list and called her cell phone. When she answered, he couldn't contain himself. "Want to celebrate tonight?"

"Celebrate?" Her voice was a mix of excitement and curiosity.

Along with her voice, he heard a buzz of noise. "Where are you?"

"Grocery shopping. But you haven't told me what you want to celebrate."

Her persistence didn't sway him. "How about going out to dinner? Something with the girls."

"Ross." She chuckled. "Why are you avoiding my question?"

He gave up trying to surprise her later and offered a quick explanation of what Dr. Timmons had said.

"That's wonderful. Something new to pray about." Excitement brightened her voice.

"I keep reminding myself that the decision hasn't been made yet, but I feel it in my heart that it will be good news." He closed his eyes a moment, drawing in the reality. Peyton might be able to live a normal life. He fought back tears of joy. "So what about celebrating?"

"I'm at the checkout now."

He heard the rustle of noise.

"Come to the house and we'll figure out something."

Ross pictured her rushing through her shopping and putting groceries away. "Let's do this. You've never been to my house and it's time you came over. Don't rush. Come when you're ready. I don't live that far from you."

She chuckled. "You heard my harried voice, didn't you?" Another rustling sound. "Thanks."

He gave her his address and when the call ended, he smiled and looked at Peyton. "They'll come to our house and then decide."

She gave a nod.

He turned on the ignition and pulled away from the hospital. Why hadn't he ever invited Kelsey to his home? The only answer he could think of was he'd taken small steps in their relationship. He feared losing the friendship if she suspected he would like more than that. Dumb, now that he thought about it.

"Daddy?"

His pulse skipped hearing Peyton's voice. His mind had been miles away. "What?"

"Will I get better if I can have the new medication?" Her voice filled with great hope.

He reached over and rested his hand on her arm. "Peyton, we can hope and pray. When the doctor told us about it, I was so excited, and yet I'm scared, too. But I feel right in here..." He shifted his hand to his heart. "That they'll approve it for you."

She rested her hand over his. "I love you, Daddy."

His bursting heart compressed as he fought the tears brimming in his eyes. "I love you, too, Peyton. More than you'll ever know." He gave her arm a pat. "Now, let's think of what we can do tonight."

She grinned. "Pizza."

"Okay, pizza it is."

Kelsey pulled into the driveway and gazed at Ross's lovely house. She had never pictured where he lived, which surprised her, and what she saw surprised her even more. A long porch graced the front of his home, leaving a recessed wing on each side displaying a window box. She could picture them filled with summer flowers. The porch was adorned with four double columns, reminding her of a plantation house. Two classic arched windows with French panes sat low on each side of the front door, featuring the same glass arch as the frame. She could imagine the wonderful sunlight filtering into the rooms.

She pushed opened the car door, and Lucy flung hers wide. "This is pretty."

She pointed to the three dormers with the same arched French-pane windows. *Charming* is the word that struck her. They headed up the brick walk with matching steps leading to the porch.

"I wonder which room is Peyton's." She stood back and eyed the dormers.

Kelsey shrugged. "We'll find out tonight."

Lucy tittered as she rang the doorbell.

Ross appeared with a smile that wove through Kelsey's chest. "Welcome."

She stepped inside the foyer. "This is a lovely place, and look here." She stopped in the dining-room doorway.

"As you can guess, we mainly eat in the kitchen." He motioned behind him. "Tonight we'll use the dining room."

She spun around. "Don't tell me you cooked." She sniffed the air and found no hint of food cooking.

"How does pizza sound?"

Lucy clapped her hands. "Pizza!"

He gave her a quick squeeze. "It should be here soon."

He'd never hugged Lucy before and Kelsey smiled, realizing how good it seemed.

"Have a seat." He motioned through the archway. "Peyton's in her room. I'll call her." He hurried past her into the room and vanished down another hallway.

She followed him into the great room, very large with a staircase leading up to the second floor, a fireplace, wet bar and another wide porch she saw through the window.

The layout was much like her house but larger. Lucy hurried across the room and pressed her nose against the window, but her greatest interest seemed to be in the direction Ross had gone.

Kelsey didn't sit. Instead she wandered through the doorway into an expansive kitchen with a breakfast nook and beyond an even larger keeping room where Ross placed his easy chairs and television. She loved it and nestled into one of the easy chairs, imagining what life would be like if she had such a room.

The doorbell rang, and she rose. As she stepped back into the great room, Ross headed toward her empty-handed. He grinned and beckoned her to follow. Then she remembered.

They settled around the dining-room table with pizza and salad. Conversation dwindled as they ate, but she noticed that Peyton and Lucy had chosen to sit next to each other. When they finished, Kelsey put her thoughts into words. "My sister is coming for a visit at the end of this month. I think she'll be here for Lucy's birthday."

"You're having a birthday?" Peyton looked at Lucy with interest.

She nodded. "On May 20."

Peyton looked curious. "Will you have a party?"

Lucy shrugged. "Will I, Mom?"

"I had plans in mind, but now your aunt wants to do something with you on your birthday."

"Aunt Audrey?" She wrinkled her nose. "Mom, she's too picky, and—"

Kelsey scowled back. "We'll talk about this later, okay?"

She gave a huff. "It's always talk later."

From the tone of her voice, Kelsey recognized a very iffy acceptance, but it worked. Audrey was opinionated. Lucy was right about that. Steering away from that conversation, she pushed her plate aside. "So what are we going to do now?"

"Peyton said she'd like to stay home and play games." Ross's neck swiveled, eyeing them.

Lucy clapped her hands. "I love games."

Peyton scooted back in her chair and beckoned to Lucy. "Let's pick out some games."

Lucy slid from her chair, unfazed by Peyton's surprise invitation, and followed her out of the room.

As she went through the doorway, Kelsey heard her mention Chinese checkers. Kelsey chuckled. "She's wanted to play since she brought them home. She even put the game in the car, just in case."

"Sounds fine with me." Ross rose and gathered the pizza boxes.

"Peyton should choose. It's her celebration." She rose and placed the plates and silverware into a stack. "Let me help you."

He strode to the kitchen and Kelsey followed, carrying what she could. She set the plates on the counter and turned on the tap to rinse them, but Ross's arm slid around her and drew her toward him. She looked into his eyes, wondering.

"Can you believe this?"

Believe? "You mean Peyton and Lucy?"

"Yes. They were talking like two friends."

Kelsey grinned. "It's about time."

He chuckled, but his expression changed. "I've hoped for this for so long, because it means..."

His eyes captured hers and he didn't have to continue. Kelsey knew what he was thinking. "It's nice to see."

"I...I've wondered where our friendship might lead, and I know we have so many issues to deal with, but..."

She nodded, waiting for him to continue. He didn't. Instead he drew closer, his eyes searching hers until he lowered his mouth to her lips. His touch rolled through her. Her heartbeat quickened as his warm lips sought hers with a tender abandon. When he drew back, she inched open her eyes, thinking she might be dreaming.

Ross grinned, his face flushed. "I've wanted to do that forever."

Heat crept up her neck, realizing she wanted the same things.

Ross brushed his hand across her cheek. "I think you know what I started to say. I want more of our relationship. I'd like to see where this will go for us."

Yes, part of her wanted a relationship. She wanted to feel whole again—God planned life in twos. She saw it everywhere. Yet admitting it made it too real. One positive incident with the girls didn't resolve all their issues. She put a clamp on her negativity. "I'd like that too, Ross."

"Dad?"

They flew apart as the girls rushed into the room. "We're going to play Lucy's game."

He grinned and eased farther away. "Chinese checkers."

She nodded.

But Lucy seemed less excited, and Kelsey wondered why. "Do you want to go to the car and get the game?"

"I guess."

"I'll get my car keys." She strode through the kitchen doorway with Lucy on her heels, relieved when Ross and Peyton stayed behind. She heard him rinsing dishes as she grabbed her purse and guided Lucy to the door. Before she opened it, she faced Lucy. "What's wrong?"

"How come she gets the big bedroom?"

Befuddled, Kelsey tried to decipher her question. "This is a bigger house than ours."

Lucy shook her head. "She has the master bedroom. Her dad gave it to her because she's sick." Her expression hardened. "I'm sick, and I don't have a special bedroom."

"Lucy, I don't know why." She pictured the house from

the outside. "Maybe most of the bedrooms are upstairs, and you know that Peyton has a heart condition."

"I have tumors, Mom. Her dad gave her his room, and she made sure I knew it."

Tension rammed up Kelsey's spine. So much for two girls getting along. "Maybe she's proud that her dad did something special for her."

Lucy rolled her eyes.

Ross's kiss lingered on her lips, but hope slithered to her toes. "Lucy, I don't have all the answers." She tugged open the front door and handed her the keys. "Go and get the game."

Lucy gave her a pouty look and huffed off.

The master bedroom. Disappointment wrenched her hopes. Finally, the two had made progress, but one small incident—a bedroom—edged out their camaraderie. She'd never expected Lucy to be competitive over something so petty. Yes, with games, but not this. Not a bedroom.

The progress shriveled as Ross's hopeful admission fluttered away. *I'd like to see where this will go for us.* Once again, she could see where it was going. Nowhere.

Chapter Eleven

"Good meeting." Ross pushed open the Senior Center door for Kelsey. The stress that tightened her face concerned him. "It was nice seeing a couple more men in the mix." He eyed her again, and she appeared miles away. "Can you sense if the women are accepting the male invasion?"

Instead of grinning or snapping back a witty response, she gave him a serious look. "I think they're doing fine with it. I don't see that it's changed the atmosphere. I've even thought the women might be benefiting from a male perspective."

"Good to hear. I would have felt rotten if my asking to join MOSK ruined the camaraderie. It's obviously important to everyone there." He dug into his pocket and searched for his car keys. "Everyone's dealing with too much stress."

She nodded, staring at the ground as she walked. "We are."

"Kelsey, is something wrong?"

Her head jerked up, and she faltered. "Nothing important."

He questioned her response. "Is Lucy okay?"

"She's fine." Her frown deepened.

"If that's not bothering you, I know something is." He placed his hand on her arm to slow her. "Can I help?"

She halted and released a stream of breath. "I told you I'm fine."

Ross slipped his hand to her shoulder. "I don't think so." He tilted her chin wanting to look into her eyes. They said so much. "I've only known you for a few months, but that doesn't mean I can't tell when something's bothering you. I've always noticed when you're stressed or on edge no matter how you try to hide it, and I feel that now. If it's something I did, I wish you'd—"

"I'm distracted today, I guess. Lucy's been a little snippy at home, and it's upsetting me. My sister called last night. They'll be here for Lucy's birthday. Naturally, Audrey's arriving on a Tuesday of all days, and I'm not sure what I'll do about the MOSK meeting. Then Lucy's facing an appointment with her physician about this year's follow-up tests. Her previous tests were six months ago so he'll compare the two and…"

"And you're worried about that."

"It's a combination of things." She shrugged. "I'd wanted to surprise Lucy with something special on her birthday, and now my sister will be here, which means she'll take charge. She always does."

She'd made other innuendos about her sister, but he hadn't caught on until today. "I take it you don't get along well."

"No, we do, but she's one of those people who wants to take over, and you know me—"

"You're a good leader, but I know you prefer to be a peacemaker." He'd spotted that the day he met her. "Before she arrives, make plans and tell her what they are."

She gave a hopeless grin. "She already announced on the phone twice that she wanted to plan something."

Tension seeped from Ross's shoulders. If the problem was her sister, he could accept that. At least it didn't involve something he'd done. "Give Lucy two celebrations. Yours and hers."

"I should just deal with it." Kelsey grinned, but he could see that she'd forced it. "I'm just edgy, as you said."

"I've been worried, too."

She looked surprised. "You didn't say anything about that at the meeting."

"No, I guess I didn't want to delve into it now, until I knew for sure."

Her brow furrowed. "You're confusing me."

"I'm confusing myself." He managed a grin. "Dr. Timmons's office called, and he wants us to go in to talk. I'm sure it's about the new medication. It's either good news or bad news, and I would almost rather not know."

Kelsey eyes widened. "Now you're not making sense."

"If it's bad news, I'll be disappointed, probably more like discouraged, because I've thought about it so much and how it will make a difference in Peyton's life. Bad news means that dreams would be over the fence."

"Why are you thinking about bad news? You want good news, naturally."

Nothing made sense lately. "If it's good news, I'm still worried if it doesn't work or if it causes some other problem. It's a new drug, he said. Just approved." He rubbed the back of his neck, trying to release the tension. "Dr. Timmons wouldn't give me an opinion on the medication without consultation with other specialists. Somehow that doesn't smack of confidence."

"To me it sounds like an excellent doctor who cares enough about his patient to want to offer the best opinion possible." She shook her head. "Ross, how many times have you told me to have faith and to think positive?"

The reminder jarred him. Emotions tangled around his mind and heart, and he faced his own failing. "Easier said than done, I guess."

She leaned into him. "I'll pray for good news and good results."

He slipped his arm around her shoulder. "Thanks. I suppose I should stop worrying and do the same."

"You should. Worrying doesn't get either of us anywhere." She adjusted her shoulder bag. "I need to be on my way."

He studied her, still seeing something in her eyes. "I'll call you." She lifted her hand in a wave and headed toward her car.

Before he took a step, he snapped his fingers. "Kelsey."

She glanced over her shoulder and stopped.

He drew closer. "I've been meaning to ask you if you'd like to attend church with us on Easter. Maybe we could have dinner together…unless you have other plans."

She gave a quick shake of her head. "No other plans."

An unreadable expression washed over her face. "Is this a bad idea?" he asked.

"No, but it just struck me that I rarely go to church anymore. You know I'm a Christian, but after Doug walked out and Lucy became so ill…I don't know." She looked puzzled. "I suppose I didn't want to go to church alone without Doug, and then I began to feel that God had let me down." She lifted her wide eyes to him. "I know better, but that's what I felt."

"Then taking the step on Easter seems perfect."

She nodded, but he wasn't sure she meant it.

"You know God's forgiven you for those thoughts." He managed to grin. "Now that's something to celebrate." He hoped she'd grin back.

She didn't. "Forgiveness." Her gaze drifted skyward. "Forgive us our trespasses as we forgive those who trespass against us." She wrapped her arms around her body. "How can I pray that?"

"Pray it, Kelsey, and pray that the Lord gives you a heart to forgive. It can happen."

She nodded, her face tense with thought as she took a step backward. "I need to run some errands before Lucy's out of school. Let's talk about Easter later."

Later. He watched her hurry off to her car as an empty feeling swept over him.

His muddied mind went back to the celebration at his house five days ago. He'd sensed a distance between him and Kelsey at the end of the evening, and today he still noticed something different about her. Only a feeling, but the romance that had grown now seemed to take a back seat, and it worried him. He'd asked the question before. Could two people with seriously ill children find happiness together? He'd taken it on faith that with God all things were possible and he'd sensed that their meeting was God-directed. But maybe he'd been wrong.

Kelsey stood in the kitchen, wrapped in the scent of baked ham and cheesy potatoes. Though she'd struggled with accepting Ross's invitation, she found herself saying yes and invited them to dinner. Ross's voice let her know she'd brightened his day. The past couple weeks, she had too much on her mind. Yes, her sister's visit always set her on edge. She loved Audrey, but they didn't always agree. Anticipating Lucy's prognosis from the latest tests preoccupied her until they met with the specialist, but Lucy's behavior upset her the most.

Peyton's bedroom began the problem. At first she scolded Lucy about being envious and competitive, but then the bedroom issue took another turn. Ross loved his daughter and worried about her. Having her climb the stairs every day—many times a day—also made sense, but he had a smaller bedroom on the first floor that he used. Why did he give her the master bedroom? She suspected it was Peyton's whining. Parents tried to make up for other issues by overcompensating in the wrong direction.

This kind of issue plagued her every time. Lucy's illness was life-threatening. Multiple tumors could mean a life of fighting to survive and not winning the battle. Peyton's illness had the same possibility, but catering to her wouldn't sit well with Kelsey. Not one bit. She felt hopeless.

Without warning, the morning's Easter worship service washed over her. Of all things, the pastor had talked about forgiveness and mercy and God's ultimate sacrifice of giving His son up to death for sinners. Forgiveness. Forgiving. Being forgiven. She knew all this, but knowing it didn't make it easy. He said that even though believers struggled and faltered, God answered their prayers, just like a parent who provides for his children's needs. Ross did the same thing. To him, the bedroom provided what his child needed. But…

The pastor's words rattled around in her head. As she'd listened, she grasped for that peace and understanding he talked about. God answered prayer, and she too often failed to ask. She clung to bitterness when compassion was the answer. Even now, she harbored concerns about Ross and allowed them to taint their relationship. She shook her head, amazed at how easily she stumbled.

Boiling water spattered from the pot, jolting her from her thoughts. She hurried to the stove, pulled it off and lowered the flame. She lifted the lid to check the vegetables. Nearly done. Kelsey turned off the burner and slipped the dinner rolls into the oven.

Ross's voice filtered through the doorway. It sounded as if he'd been carrying the brunt of the threesome's conversation. Though Peyton and Lucy had spoken, Kelsey sensed that her lecture had failed, and she was disappointed seeing Lucy allow envy—or was it pride?—to steal her usual good spirit. She would deal with it later.

She slipped into the dining room with the salad and dressing. The aromas titillated her stomach. No doubt everyone was ready to eat. Remembering her homemade chunky applesauce, she headed back into the kitchen. As she came through the doorway, Ross was standing near the stove.

"There you are." He rubbed his belly. "Are we almost ready?"

She couldn't help but grin. "The smell is taunting, isn't it?"

He gazed toward the ham. "Would you like me to carve?"

One job she wouldn't have to do. "You don't have to ask twice." She pointed to the electric knife she'd already plugged in and the cutting board against the wall. "Here you go." She slapped two pot holders into his hands, then opened the oven door and stepped back. "Start carving."

Ross lifted the roaster from the heat, the sweet, spicy fragrance hovering in the air. "Wonderful. What am I smelling?"

"Cloves and ginger ale. My secret ingredients."

He chuckled, and while he sliced the ham, she carried the potato-cheese casserole and a bowl of mixed vegetables to the table.

"What do you think?" Ross stepped back when she returned and pointed to the pile of ham. "Enough?"

She nodded. "If you'll put that on the table, I'll call the girls."

His eyebrows raised. "Speaking of the girls, I'm really discouraged."

She didn't have to ask.

"For once Peyton's making a little effort to be pleasant, but Lucy's not helping. That's really odd, don't you think?"

The question hung in the air, and Kelsey's answer lodged in her throat.

Ross frowned. "What do you know that I don't?"

Her mind flew, trying to decide how to approach the topic without ruining the day. *Temper your comment* flashed through her mind. "Lucy's competitive, as you know. I think she's a bit irked that Peyton has the master bedroom."

"What?" Disbelief registered on his face.

If he knew anything about women—or Lucy—he should understand. "She wasn't given the master bedroom here when she was diagnosed with a life-threatening disease."

His arm swung out in a large arc. "Kelsey, your house is on one floor. Lucy didn't have to climb stairs." He shook his head. "Anyway, Lucy's illness has nothing to do with her heart."

"Her brain is affected. It's what controls almost everything in her body."

"Yes, but…" He looked startled.

"You have two bedrooms on the first floor, and Lucy knows that." She monitored her volume. "You manage just fine using the guestroom. Why can't Peyton?" The question rang with her irritation, and she hurried to soften her comment. "That's what Lucy wants to know." But so did she. The whole situation overwhelmed her. This issue had little to do with a bedroom. It reminded her of the difficulty they faced—two who might never see eye to eye.

"She'd lost a mother and then found out she had the same disease. I wanted to…" He looked exasperated.

Ross didn't understand. "Lucy grew up without much of a father, too." She brushed the words away. "Forget it. I've talked to Lucy, and I'll talk with her again. She'll get over it." But Kelsey sensed that this might be only the beginning.

"I'm sorry you feel that way."

She shook her head. "Peyton's your daughter, Ross. You have the right to coddle her any way you choose. She's very ill. I understand that."

"Mom." Lucy darted into the room. "I'm starving. When are we gonna eat?"

Grateful for the interruption, she monitored her voice. "Right now. Tell Peyton, okay?"

Lucy spun around and called out to Peyton as she hurried back into the living room.

Kelsey pulled the dinner rolls from the oven, and once they settled around the table, Ross said the blessing. The food circled the table, and they filled their plates. Conversation lulled as they slivered their ham and dug into the cheesy potatoes, and she was grateful. She'd set off a fire that could turn into a blaze. Why hadn't she kept her mouth shut and let it go? Her comment served no purpose but to vent her own upset.

Ross had become an important part of her life. Their relationship had grown deeper. His kiss had excited her and made her feel like a woman again. His kindness and concern made even her parents' support look weak. Yet she'd uttered words ringing with sarcasm.

She lifted her gaze from her plate and studied his face. He looked deep in thought. Had she let her frustration ruin her chance for happiness? Ross had been the first man to arouse her sense of femininity and stir her emotions. She lowered her gaze. *What have I done?*

"I don't understand." Kelsey's hand knotted in her lap. "Why does Lucy need another test?"

"Two tests, Mrs. Rhodes." He looked at her. "I've studied her last MRI and I see something I'd like to view more carefully." His gaze drifted to Lucy. "You want to be well, I know, Lucy, so you're willing to have a couple more tests."

She glanced at her mother, then eyed Dr. Bryant. "What kind of test?"

His grin looked guarded. "Nothing that will hurt or keep you in the hospital."

Relief flooded her face. "Okay."

"You've had the PET scan before. You'll get a low-dose injection of radioactive sugar followed by the scan."

Lucy nodded. "I remember."

Kelsey's stomach knotted. He'd spotted something, or he wouldn't do this. She wanted to know, but did she want Lucy to hear what was wrong? The muscles in her neck tightened.

"The other test is one Lucy's never had." He looked at Kelsey, then gazed at the paperwork on his desk. "This is another form of brain MRI. A fairly new process called fMRI, which means functional magnetic resonance imaging. The procedure is very similar to your regular MRI."

Kelsey's heart constricted. "What is this for, doctor?"

He paused a moment, his eyes focused on the paperwork. "We realized that Lucy's lesion has increased since her last brain MRI. I'd like to check it out and see what's happening there."

Kelsey closed her eyes, not wanting to know the answer to her question. "Why would this happen?"

"That's what we want to learn from the tests. It's likely scar tissue and that's always a problem. You know we have to keep that to a minimum."

"And if it's not that?"

He released a sigh. "It could be a small tumor."

"No." Lucy's voice burst from her. "I don't want to go through all that again."

"I know, Lucy. I know. But this is to keep you healthy. We can take care of an early problem. You have to be happy we spotted it before it turned into something more serious."

"But will they ever stop?"

Lucy's plaintive plea rent Kelsey's heart. She slipped her arm around Lucy's shoulder. "These tests may show that you're fine. Let's just get them over with, okay?"

She gave a slow nod.

"I'll get the tests scheduled for you, and I'll give you a call."

Kelsey nodded as he closed the file and then stood. She beckoned Lucy to rise.

Dr. Bryant gave Lucy a tender look. "We'll fix whatever needs fixing, Lucy, and hopefully, it's nothing at all."

"I don't have much choice, do I?"

Her soft response sounded pitiful, and Kelsey struggled to keep her wits about her. "Let's go." She guided Lucy through the door and down the hallway, longing to call Ross, but she stopped herself. If the relationship ends… Sadness swept over her. If it ended, she'd have to find her solace and support somewhere else. She gazed at Lucy's stressed face. Today she needed to talk with someone. Images rifled through her mind. Lexie. After they were home, she would call her. Lexie listened well and understood. That's what she needed.

Chapter Twelve

"We're anxious to hear what you've decided." Ross kept his hands in his lap, fearing that his apprehension would show.

Dr. Timmons looked over the top of his glasses. "This will be your decision, Mr. Salburg, but I think we have a good chance with this new medication."

"Really?" The tremors in his hands became more obvious, and he wove his fingers even tighter in his lap. "What does this mean?"

The specialist flipped open a file and studied it a moment. "I consulted with a number of heart specialists who have more experience with the new medication than I have. Two of them were ones who received it first to help identify the successes and failures in using it." He lifted his gaze to Ross. "And yes, we can have failures, but these aren't life-threatening. They just don't do the job we'd hoped."

That's what Ross feared—failure—and that meant disappointment. Discouragement always set him back worse than anything else. Hope could too easily be dampened by the reality of another unsuccessful attempt. "But you think this will work for Peyton?"

Timmons nodded. "The condition of her heart is statistically more apt to experience improvement with the medication than not."

Air drained from Ross's lungs. "Then that's good news."

"Yes. The medication is expensive and new, so it means dealing with your insurance company. We'll send them an explanation and hope they will approve it."

Insurance. The only thing Ross cared about was seeing his daughter healthy. "If not, I could pay for it myself."

The specialist's head jerked upward. "We're talking thousands per month. Let's hope your insurance covers it."

Thousands. His mind darted from solution to solution. But reality told him that while he made a decent living, thousands would run out in time, and then what?

"Mr. Salburg, please don't think this is hopeless. We have good statistics, and we'll contact your insurance company with the request. If they refuse, then we'll see how we might deal with it."

Hope with an addendum. He wanted to burst with joy, but that didn't happen. "How long will it take to get a response?"

"I'll get the information ready today, and then it's up to them. I hope within a couple of weeks." He gave Peyton a hopeful look. "But don't be disappointed if they refuse. They sometimes do that, and we'll appeal the case."

Ross's shoulders slumped as he rose. "Thank you." He extended his hand, and Timmons grasped it.

"We'll let you know as soon as we hear anything."

Ross nodded, wrapped his arm around Peyton's shoulders and left the room. As they headed outside, he realized how much Peyton had grown in the past few months. Once she'd reached the top of his elbow, and today her head was close to his shoulder. Twelve. A young woman soon. The thought made him cringe. He needed to talk with her, and he dreaded it—the talk her mother should give, not her father. He pressed his lips together, wishing he could find the courage today.

"What do you think, Peyton? You're quiet."

"I want to get better, and I keep praying that this will work. Now I have to pray for the insurance to cover it." She shook her head. "Dad, does anything ever happen in life that is problem-free?"

"Some things do." He drew her closer to his side. "But count on problems sometimes. They happen to good people."

"Like us?"

He nodded. "Yes, people like us." Kelsey's face flashed before him. She'd hurt him the other night, and he didn't know how to resolve that problem, either.

"But maybe it will work out, and I'll get better. Then our lives will be good." She tilted her head toward him, her eyes asking. "Right?"

"Right. We'll keep praying that God has good things in store for us."

Her step seemed lighter as they headed into the parking lot, but Ross's didn't. Normally he'd call Kelsey to tell her the results of this visit, but now he wondered where they stood. He hadn't called her since Easter, trying to get his head on straight. He still prickled from her comments. She seemed to think he coddled Peyton. That was the word she'd used. *Coddled.* How do you not focus on a sick child? How do you not try to ease her suffering and fear with special treatment? Kelsey wasn't hard-hearted. He knew that. So what was going on with her? That's what he wanted to know.

Kelsey folded her notes from the MOSK meeting and tucked them into her notebook while Lexie waited beside the door. When she turned, Lexie opened her arms.

"I'm really sorry about the news, Kelsey."

Her chest tightened. "So am I, but I'm trying to stay positive."

"You should, because the doctor said he didn't know for sure, and it could be nothing." She slipped her arm around her shoulders. "No Ross today, either. I'm surprised. He seems to get a lot out of the meetings. He sometimes talks to Ethan about it."

She nodded, trying to hold back the remorse she felt. She knew she shouldn't have said a word about the bedroom. Not only what she said to Ross, but how she said it came across so wrong.

"I'm sure he hated to tell you his good news when you'd just gotten something new to worry about."

Good news. Her head jerked upward. "What good news?"

Lexie's arm slipped from her back. "What? Are you telling me you haven't talked with him?"

"Not in a couple of days." More than a couple. Her depression deepened.

Lexie's eyes narrowed and a frown slid to her face. "An argument?"

She shrugged. "Not an argument really. Just words, but words I shouldn't have said."

"I'm sorry, Kelsey." She shook her head. "Want to talk about it?"

She bit her lip. She hated to talk about it because it showed her nasty side, and it shamed her. But Lexie had a good head, so she decided to tell her what had happened.

Lexie stood a moment, digesting her explanation. "What happened to the woman who can soothe a raging lion?"

"I guess I'm better at soothing lions than at taking care of my own conduct. I'm really sorry about what I said, but that's how I felt that day. Lucy kept bringing it up and making me feel as if I'm not a good mother, because I didn't give her my bedroom. I—"

"You said what's important. You're sorry."

Kelsey closed her eyes and pondered what Lexie said. "I am, but within it all, there is some truth."

"Truth is sometimes in the eyes of the beholder."

"I thought that was beauty." She tried to grin, but it didn't happen.

"It's the same thing, isn't it? Truth. Beauty. It's our perspective. Ross did what he felt he needed to do for his daughter. It was a kind thing. We criticize people for being cruel and unloving to their children. Ross treats his daughter the way Jesus said. Do unto others as you would have them do unto you."

The sting of Lexie's comment hit home. "You're right."

"And it's something he can undo."

"In time."

Kelsey heart skipped. "What's his good news?" She listened as Lexie told her about the new medication that could make a huge difference in Peyton's life. As the words sank in, her spirit lifted with hope for Ross's daughter. The girl needed something good in her life. Losing a mother and being stricken with the same disease that took her assailed Kelsey with full force. A child bearing the weight of so much difficulty. But now she had hope. She could win the battle. "I'm glad you told me. Even if he's upset with me, I want him to know how happy I am."

"That's the right thing to do."

It was. She reached up and snapped off the meeting-room light. "I'll call him when I get home. My sister's due any minute, and I hate to keep her waiting."

"No, you don't want to do that." She chuckled.

Lexie had heard Kelsey's complaints about her sister a few times, and that's another thing Kelsey sometimes felt sad about. She should try to lighten up.

She waved to Lexie as she slipped into her car, reviewing what she should say to Ross and wondering when she could talk to him if her sister was already there.

Relief washed through her when she pulled down her street and saw her driveway empty. Hopefully, she would have a few minutes before Audrey arrived. She glanced at her watch, pleased that it wasn't as late as she thought. The conversation with Lexie must have been shorter than it seemed.

She headed inside and dropped her purse and notebook on the kitchen counter, grabbed a glass of water and headed for the phone, but it rang before she could dial. Her pulse skipped, envisioning that the caller was Ross. Instead, she recognized the doctor's office and answered.

"Mrs. Rhodes, Lucy's tests are set for Monday, May 30. The fMRI will be first and then the PET scan is scheduled. You should be at the hospital by nine. I hope this works for you."

"That's fine. We'll be there." She hung up the phone, struck by the reality of the call. Lucy facing more serious tests. She'd never wanted to go through this again. Tears sprang into her eyes, tears she'd kept buried. But not today.

She crossed the room and reached for a napkin to wipe away the moisture. When her vision cleared, she looked at the clock. She barely had time to call. Audrey could arrive any second, but she didn't want to wait any longer. As she approached the telephone, it rang again, and eyeing the number, her heart constricted. Ross. He'd called despite her unpleasant comments. Her fingers shook as she gripped the headset. "Ross."

"Kelsey, no matter how angry you are at me, you should have called me."

Tears welled in her eyes. "I…" She choked back a sob. "I'm sorry and…" No words expressed the dismal feelings smothering her. "I'd planned to call you when I got in. My sister's due any minute, but I heard about Peyton's medicine. I'm so happy. I thank God."

"I'm glad." His voice had softened, and within it, she heard hesitation. "Tell me about Lucy."

Her throat compressed as she told him. He'd been her source of security, her support, these past few months, and she missed that. She missed him.

"This tears me up. How could this happen? She's been doing so well. A year. More than a year."

"I know, and it's the uncertainty that puts me on edge." She sank into a chair. "Remember when you told me about the medicine? You were afraid that the doctor wouldn't feel it was right for Peyton, and you feared it might be, because you still faced the indefinite results." She closed her eyes. "I guess that's how I feel. I pray it's nothing. A misreading. A fluke in the image." She dragged in a breath. "Not another tumor. I don't think I could bear it."

"I understand. Even now we have no guarantee about the insurance or the success. It's still up in the air." She listened as he explained the insurance situation, asking herself what would she do if Lucy's treatments cost hundreds of thousands that weren't covered. The answer was clear. As Ross said, she would do anything. Sell her house. Whatever it took.

"God can make anything happen, Ross. We just have to pray."

"Unceasingly."

How many times had she told herself that? "And we will."

Ross hesitated. "So where do we stand? I need to see you." His plea etched with apprehension.

Kelsey winced at the sound. Her comment had wounded him, and yet her concern had been real. They needed time, but how? Her sister would arrive at any moment. She had no idea what Lucy's latest problem would do to her. And Lucy's birthday. She tried to concentrate, but just then a car door sounded outside.

"Ross, I think Audrey's here. I'll call you later so we can resolve this, okay?"

"Resolve us or take time to talk?" Sadness emanated from his tone.

"Not us. I mean find time to talk." She heard the door rattle. "I have to go. She's here, but I'll call." She hung up, dashed to the door and flung it open.

Audrey's eyes widened. "I thought you weren't home."

"I was on the phone. Sorry." Kelsey pushed the door open. "Where's Jeff?"

"At his meetings. I'll pick him up before the party." Audrey stepped inside pulling a carry-on bag. "I've been upset since we last spoke. I'm so sorry about Lucy." She drew Kelsey into an embrace. "How's she taking it?"

"Better than I am, I think." She motioned for Audrey to come inside. "Lucy focuses on the positive side of things. She's upset, but she bounces back fast."

Audrey looked around. "She's not here?"

"No. School won't be out for another hour and a half."

"Good. That gives us time to talk about her birthday." Audrey grabbed her bag, rolled it into the great room and paused by the stairs. "Which bedroom?"

"Take the biggest one at the top of the stairs."

She gave her an okay sign and headed toward the guest room. Kelsey drew in a breath and continued to the kitchen. She turned on water for tea—her sister's favorite—then leaned her back against the cabinet. She ached inside since talking to Ross. She'd hurt him, and it was wrong. Being unkind had never been her way, but she'd done exactly that. Her tone of voice had taken her words to another level. She'd known it the moment they flew from her mouth. Sarcasm had taken over, and her usual peacemaker's approach had vanished.

How could she have done that to someone who meant so much to her? She realized it now, facing what she'd done. She'd missed him the past few days. They'd always talked nearly every day, even when they didn't have time to see each other. She laughed at how many times the phone rang in the middle of her workday. But she loved the interruption.

Now she had to put him off again with Audrey's arrival. Such rotten timing.

Kelsey pulled herself back from the counter edge and lifted out two mugs and dessert plates. She dropped two tea bags in the cups and opened up the plastic container filled with home-baked peanut butter cookies with a chocolate kiss pressed into the center. Also her sister's favorite. As she turned, Audrey stepped into the kitchen. "Did you find everything? I set out fresh towels for you."

"Everything's fine." She stepped closer. "What's on the plate?" She eyed the cookies and grinned. "You remembered."

"How could I forget? Let's sit over there." She motioned to the breakfast table and waited for Audrey to go ahead. She set down the cookies and returned to the kitchen counter to prepare the tea. "So what do you have in mind for Lucy's birthday?"

"Something fun."

She could tell that Audrey had already bitten into a cookie. "That sounds mysterious."

Audrey chuckled. "It's something I loved to do as a kid."

Kelsey's mind stretched into her childhood. Audrey liked to do many things and nothing struck her. "What?"

"Roller skating."

The water for tea spewed from the kettle and Kelsey poured it into the mugs. Roller skating. Lucy had only gone skating a couple of times, although she did okay, but what about Peyton? The question knotted in her throat. "That's a stra—unusual idea."

"Why? Kids love to skate. At least they do in Traverse City."

Kelsey jammed her mouth closed. "Your idea's different. I can say that." She lifted a mug in each hand, managed a pleasant expression and walked back to her sister. "Do you still skate?" She couldn't imagine, but the idea was way outside the box as far as she was concerned. And Peyton was still an issue.

"No, but it's like riding a bicycle, I would think." Audrey grasped the mug and took a sip. "What had you planned?"

Kelsey sank into a chair, measuring her words. "Nothing. I was waiting for your idea."

"It's not just roller skating. I made reservations to eat at Buca di Beppo. Italian and fun. Have you been there?"

"No, but I've heard of it. Lucy loves Italian food."

"I remembered. And they bring out a birthday cake with all the waiters singing. She'll be thrilled." Audrey gazed at her a moment. "So what do you think?"

Kelsey couldn't disagree. "It'll be fun." Peyton's face edged into her mind, no matter how hard she tried to push it out. Telling her sister about Ross might elicit an enthusiastic response, but if she learned about Peyton, that could be another story. Not inviting them wasn't the answer. Yet now she faced the roller-skating issue.

She roused her courage. "Audrey, I think the restaurant is great. Lucy will love it, but I have qualms about roller skating."

Audrey's eyes widened. "Why?"

Why? Kelsey felt the truth bustle into her mind. She couldn't lie, but maybe she could mention that Lucy doesn't really roller skate. "I have a friend that I planned to invite to Lucy's birthday."

Audrey arched a brow. "Friend?" She tilted her head. "Female friend or..." A grin hinted on her lips.

"Ross. His name is Ross Salburg."

She clapped her hands together, brushed the crumbs from her lips and bounced up, planting a kiss on Kelsey's cheek. "Really? Someone special?"

Play it down. The words popped into her mind. She pushed them back. "Special but nothing serious yet."

Audrey drew her from the chair for a hug. "*Yet.* That sounds hopeful." She eased back and eyed her sister. "Will I meet him?"

Kelsey settled into her chair. "You will, and his daughter Peyton. She's a year older than Lucy."

"Hmm? A daughter." She sank back into the seat, a thoughtful look growing on her face. "Any competition? How do they get along?"

Questions. That's what she wanted to avoid. She sank back into the chair. "Fine. Peyton's quieter than Lucy. She's had some health problems, too."

The smile faded to concern. "What kind of problems?"

"Her heart, and that's why I think maybe roller skating might not work." She studied her sister's expression and sensed that she wasn't going to relent easily. "I'd hate to leave her out."

Audrey's face became thoughtful. "Rolling around the floor on skates wouldn't be that hard on her. Let's just plan it, and hopefully she'll be able to skate. I'm really looking forward to this."

Kelsey resigned herself to going along with her sister. Dissing her plans never worked when they were young, and she knew Audrey had only polished her ability to stay firm over the years. She'd talk it over with Ross. Not wanting to stir up dissension, she nodded and let it drop.

Audrey leaned back and grew quiet, leaving Kelsey with an anxious feeling. When Audrey thought, it could mean anything. She watched as her sister pursed her lips together, then lifted her head. Kelsey pressed her back against the chair rungs for support.

"Do you really think it's wise for you to get involved with a man who has a child with a heart problem?" She leaned closer, her eyes searching Kelsey's. "Do you know what I mean? Two sick kids. What kind of life is that? Where's the romance?"

She seemed to draw closer, although she hadn't stood. Kelsey swallowed every comment that flittered through her mind. This wasn't new. Her own friend, Lexie, had suggested the same thing, but then apologized. Still she'd always be facing the possibility of a child fighting to stay alive. Her muddied mind lost all concept of communication. What could she say to make her sister happy? She couldn't deny it, because Audrey was right.

"Men and women can be friends without romance, Audrey." True but not really the case with Ross. She cared so much, and she sensed that he did, too.

"Those things are hard to control. Sometimes people become a habit. You need them for support and a sort of security, and soon you think it's love and it's not. Then what?"

What? Her relationship with Ross didn't seem like that. Not a habit. Yes, she needed his support. She realized that today, and having him by her side gave her security, but she cared about him. Not what he had to offer. Her pulse quickened, weighing her thoughts. She didn't feel that way, but maybe Ross did, and what then?

She confined the thoughts raging inside her. Asking Audrey if she'd arrived to put a downer on Kelsey's life would only stir up trouble. Assuming that her sister was worried about her, she avoided responding to her comment. "You'll meet him tonight at Lucy's party, Audrey. Then you can decide for yourself."

Audrey shrugged and grabbed another peanut-butter cookie. "Fair enough."

Fair enough. Kelsey wanted to either scream or cry.

Chapter Thirteen

~~~~~

Ross stood near the refreshment stand, watching Peyton on the roller rink. He'd been put in a touchy position, but he gave Peyton the choice. She wanted to go, and he sensed a touch of competition. Now that he had met Audrey, he understood Kelsey's problem. Though a nice woman, Audrey had a way of taking charge, even if her take-charge attitude wasn't welcome.

When Kelsey called him, he wanted to balk at the roller-skating decision, but she explained her attempt to talk her sister out of the idea with no success. If it hadn't been Lucy's birthday, he would have declined.

He eyed the rink floor, spotting Audrey and her husband, Jeff. They flew around the floor like kids. Appropriate, since most of the skaters were teens. Jeff seemed to be a sensible man but a bit intimidating. Ross's pulse stumbled when he saw Lucy skating beside Peyton. Their pace looked slower than the rest, and he guessed that Lucy was doing it for Peyton. He grinned, touched by Lucy's thoughtfulness. It more than made up for her grumbling about the bedroom, which had tripped the switch that turned her mother into the sarcastic woman he'd faced a week back.

Watching the skaters, a concern rose in his mind. Some

of them wore helmets, along with elbow and knee protectors. Peyton would be safer with protection since she was still taking coumadin. A bruise could cause undue problems while using the blood thinner. Though it was too late now, he wished he'd given skating more thought.

When he spotted Kelsey, she was standing beside the rink floor taking a few more photos. He hoped she caught a couple with the girls skating together. The positive turn of events lifted his spirit. She lowered the camera and scanned the floor before glancing over her shoulder. When she noticed him, his heart danced. She looked gorgeous in her knit top the color of spring grass, and instead of fighting her part, she'd curled her hair and it waved about her shoulders.

She headed his way, a concerned expression on her face. "Are you okay?"

He heard her question despite the music and whoosh of skates nearby and nodded. Every time he gazed at her lips, he spiraled out of control. Their one complete kiss lingered in his mind, the soft touch, the feel of her in his arms. Tonight he longed to run his fingers through her curls. Trying to keep their relationship in perspective had failed. Totally failed. She rocked him on his feet every time he looked at her. They needed to talk. Serious talk about the future. Yet every time they tried, something interrupted them. They were never alone. Tonight was yet another example.

She'd reached his side and rested her hand on his shoulder. "Are you sure?"

The touch rolled down his arm. "I'm fine." His gaze swept over her. "You look great tonight."

She gazed down at her jeans and struck a pose. "This old thing?" Then she grinned.

He chuckled at her playfulness. It had been a long time since he'd seen her lighthearted. "You'd look good in a burlap sack. I've missed you, Kelsey."

Her eyes sought his. "It's been difficult. We're both going through so much. Now my sister and—"

"And the issues we need to clear up." He motioned toward the skaters as a futile feeling billowed over him. "But when? How can we find time now?"

Her hand slipped down to his, and she squeezed it. "It's frustrating, and that's why sometimes I think what they said was right."

His stomach constricted. "Right about what?"

She closed her eyes and shook her head. "I shouldn't have said that."

He agreed. Ross didn't want to hear it. He slipped her hand into his. "We can work it out. Two are better than one." The verse lodged in his head. "What's the Bible say? Something about if you fall, the other can pick you up, and if someone overpowers you, you have someone to join you in the fight." The rest of the verse swished over him. And when they lie down together, they will keep warm. That's what he longed for in a partner, someone to hold close and cherish. His pulse hammered.

"Hey, you two."

Ross's head jerked when he heard Audrey's voice. Kelsey spun around and nearly lost her balance. He reached for her and she steadied.

Audrey grinned. "Don't tell me you're giving up? This is fun."

Ross studied the floor and couldn't see Peyton or Lucy. His heart constricted until he saw them seated in the chairs near the skating floor. "The kids are taking a break." He gave a nod toward them.

She glanced over her shoulder and chuckled. "I guess ̄ and I are the only live wires here."

He didn't comment, fearing that ̄
Everyone would prefer to

She gazed at Kelsey a moment, her focus slipping to the camera. "Did you get a shot with Ross?"

"No. I've taken all the photos."

She snatched the camera from her. "Okay, get out on that floor and let me take your picture."

"B-but…" Kelsey checked her watch. "It's getting late. What time is the dinner reservation?"

"Oh, my." Audrey eyed her watch. "I guess you're right. We need to get moving." She held up her hand. "But let me take one here anyway."

Audrey backed up as she pointed to their skates. "I want them in the photo."

Kelsey rolled her eyes, immediately thinking of Lucy. She lifted her foot, and Ross followed with a chuckle. They leaned on each other to balance, and Audrey snapped the photo.

"Okay." She dropped the camera into Kelsey's hands and waved to Jeff as she pointed to her watch. "We're ready." She swiveled and made her way to her husband.

"Sorry." Kelsey touched his arm. "Maybe later."

Her expression appeared as hopeless as he felt. "Maybe."

Their eyes met and locked. Hopeless. Helpless. He wondered if Kelsey was right. A relationship divided by so many things needed more than two people. That relationship needed the Lord.

Kelsey felt thoroughly confused. Ross had a desperate look, and it troubled her. Though he spoke about keeping their relationship firm, she sensed that on a deeper level he had begun to struggle, just as she had been doing. Sitting in the ba— Their dinner had been a treat, noisy …ily style—and a small cake …ung by some waiters. …dy fallen asleep …e, she knew their only moments to talk would end. Jeff had brought his luggage in before they left for the skating party.

Lucy loved her gifts. Ross and Peyton surprised Lucy with her first pair of earrings—expensive ones, she could tell. Talk about ecstatic—Lucy was the poster child. He'd even been thoughtful enough to check with her first to make sure she was willing to take Lucy to have her ears pierced. A gift certificate from Audrey and Jeff delighted Lucy, too. She would shop anytime she had a chance. But in the back of Kelsey's mind she wondered if the shopping would get done before she faced her latest health issue. Faith. She had to cling to it.

Her pleasant thoughts faded as Ross rolled into the driveway behind Jeff. She climbed out and opened the back seat to awaken Lucy, then ran to the entrance to unlock the door. She turned back to the car and saw Lucy weaving her way toward the house, still half asleep, as Ross carried Peyton in his arms. She'd grown since they'd met, and it reminded her of Ross's wish for a mother for Peyton. The feeling filtered past her negative thoughts and touched her heart.

She stepped away from the door and held it while Ross headed inside. "I'll put her on the sofa."

"Good idea, and grab that throw on the chair. You can cover her with that."

He continued down the hallway, and Lucy trudged in, her eyes half-closed. "Can I go to bed?"

"Certainly." Kelsey leaned down and kissed her cheek as she meandered down the hall, giving a tired wave into the living room before continuing to her bedroom door.

Kelsey wandered in and joined the others. She found Audrey and Jeff standing beside Ross. Audrey turned to Kelsey and tilted her head. "We're going to head for bed if you don't mind. It's been a long day for us driving here from Traverse City, and Jeff had that meeting right away."

"That's fine. Go right ahead." Relief eased over her. Maybe, she and Ross could have some time together.

"Kelsey." Audrey beckoned her to follow as she headed her way. "I want to show you something." Jeff didn't move, and Kelsey caught on. She wanted to talk, and if she couldn't do it here, then the talk was about Ross. She winced, anticipating more negative conversation.

In the bedroom, Audrey closed the door and faced her. "Thanks again for letting us stay here."

A fleeting moment of relief whisked through her. Maybe she was wrong. "You know you and Jeff are welcome anytime." She hoped she meant that.

"Listen, I hate to bring this up again." She motioned for Kelsey to sit on the bed.

She glanced toward the mattress but didn't move. "What's the problem?"

"Jeff and I watched you and Ross. We think if you can keep this a friendship it might work, but I doubt if you can. He's crazy about you. I see it in his face every time he looks at you."

Kelsey's heartbeat faltered. *Crazy about you.* He cared. She knew that, but crazy? A frown tugged at her face. "What are you talking about?"

"We're not blind. I think you have feelings for him, too, and I'm afraid you're going to be hurt. Both of you have children who need your total attention. Peyton seems to be sicker than you indicated. What kind of heart problem?"

She couldn't lie, but she wanted to. "Cardiomyopathy."

She gasped. "No. How horrible. You know what that means?"

"No, not in her case. It was caught early, and she's improving. Plus they now have a new medication that can make a huge difference for her. She could be like new."

Audrey looked doubtful. "But then there's Lucy. Now you're facing more tests again, and who knows what will happen."

She opened her arms, but Kelsey couldn't move. Audrey

stepped toward her and held her in an embrace. "I want you to be happy, sis, but I don't think this is the way. I think you're asking for trouble. He's a nice man, but both of you are carrying burdens, and—"

"Audrey." Kelsey pulled back. "I know what I'm facing. I told you we haven't taken any steps toward anything. We don't even have time to talk privately." She began to seethe. "So don't create problems that aren't there. Lucy will have more tests. We can only hope that it's nothing. Instead of looking for trouble, please pray with me that it is a false reading. Those things happen."

Audrey looked stricken. "I'm sorry if I upset you, and you know I pray for Lucy. I wasn't trying to cause—"

"I know you're not trying to, but don't you think I've had the same thoughts? You're my sister, and you want the best for me, but the best isn't reminding me of my difficult life. I'm tired of doing this alone, and so is Ross. Maybe we can struggle together. Remember, the Bible says two are better than one."

Audrey's face went blank. "Enough said, I suppose. I'm very tired."

"Good night, then." She forced herself to kiss her sister's cheek. "I hope you rest well, and I'll see you in the morning."

She nodded, and Kelsey made her escape. She nearly ran into Jeff in the hallway.

He grinned. "I was going to see what was keeping you girls."

"Just chatting." She gave him a hug. "Night, Jeff. Sleep well."

He slipped into the bedroom, and Kelsey released a long breath and continued back to the living room. Ross wasn't there, but she heard a sound in the kitchen. When she stepped through the doorway, he had settled at the kitchen table, a glass of water beside him. She poured a glass, too, and joined him at the table.

"So." He gazed at her, knowingly. "I'm guessing you had words with your sister."

She shrugged. "She worries about me."

"Your face says it all. She has reservations about me."

She stiffened. "She thought you were very nice."

"But she thinks you're biting off more than you can chew."

His face reflected the truth, and she couldn't hide it. "Sort of." She told him what she'd said. "I tried to block my ears."

"But you can't, Kelsey, not if people keep assuming that you and I can't deal with our problems. I said part of what I wanted to at the roller rink. Two are better than one. The Lord said it, and how can we doubt Him? Yes, we'll survive alone. We're strong and we've been doing it, but it's not what I want, and I'd like to think you would like more, too."

Her hands began to tremble as the emotion of his words burrowed into her heart. "We've handled things together for the past months. I've come to need you."

"I've come to care about you and Lucy more than I can say."

She started to tell him she cared, too, but he held up his finger to stop her.

"I'll admit I've made mistakes with Peyton. I overcompensated, and that probably set her back because she leaned on me and expected me to occupy her time. She doesn't need friends when her dad's doing everything to make her happy." His face pinched with emotion. "And I can't do that. She has to find her own happiness."

"That's ri—"

"Did you see what happened today? My chest nearly burst, and I was so proud of Lucy. Here she is facing more tests and who knows what after that, and she was skating around the rink at a snail's pace for Peyton. They were side by side. Peyton was so unsteady. I don't think she'd ever been on skates, and Lucy was her support. That's what she needs from other people. Not just me." He held up his hand as if to stop her from saying anything. "And I don't want you to think that's what makes you important to me. It's far from that. Yes, I love your help. Peyton would benefit from an adult female in her life, but I wouldn't ask you on a journey with me unless you meant more than support to me."

Kelsey's mind whirled with Ross's admission. He'd said everything but that he loved her. Words filtered through her mind, words she longed to say but instead they jammed against her heart. She couldn't make promises now. "Ross, I—"

"Before you say anything, here's my thought. If our relationship can't deal with the kinds of problems we have to face, ones that can easily be resolved and a few that will take time and prayer, then maybe we weren't meant to be more than friends. But I want to try. More than try, I want to succeed, but if you want me out of your life, tell me now. I don't want to go through this uncertain feeling every day until you decide. I'm up for it. Are you?"

Stunned, she stared at him. He'd never said so much at one time since she'd met him. Even at the MOSK meetings, he told them about the latest good and bad news, but he made his comments succinct. Her hands trembled as she reached up to touch his tense face, his look heartbreaking. She'd done that to him. "Ross, I want to take this journey with you. I know we'll have difficult times, but you're right. If we want to make this grow into something deeper and more committed, then we need to trust each other. We need to be open and, just as much, we need to be patient."

"That's all I wanted to hear." His voice quaked with emotion.

Ross rose and took her hand. Kelsey stood, tense with anticipation. He drew her into his arms and held her close, his heart beating against hers, his breathing labored. His hand rose to her cheek, his fingers brushing her skin and floating across her lips. A shiver of anticipation ran through her until he tilted her chin, and his lips met hers. His gentle mouth plied her lips with sweet kisses, his arms drew her closer, and she knew at that moment that God had ordained their meeting. For once, assurance spread through her, a comfort she'd fought but now accepted.

He eased back, his tension vanished. His eyes sought hers. "This has to be right, Kelsey."

"Completeness." The single word was all she could utter.

"We'll be patient and open from now on."

She gazed at him while her heart lifted a prayer.

Kelsey opened the door, and Ross swept in, his arm sliding around her. "Any news?" The anxious look on his face matched his voice.

"The office called today. We have an appointment on Thursday for the test results."

"That was fast."

"I know, but they wouldn't tell me a thing." Her stomach knotted. "I'm afraid it's bad news."

He gave her a squeeze. "Don't assume that. Nurses and especially receptionists can't give out information without the physician's permission. Let's pray that everything is fine."

"I have been." She motioned him inside, and he followed her to the kitchen. "Coffee?"

"No, I have an appointment in…" He gazed at his watch. "In forty minutes so I can't stay. I was close by so I thought I'd stop."

"I'm glad you did."

He bent and kissed her. The sensation rushed to her chest. Since their talk on Friday, she'd been overwhelmed by her emotions. They tilted one way, then the other—from pure joy to pure worry that she would fail. He'd offered her a journey, a trip to assure them both they could do this, and she wanted to with all her heart. Still, the old fear uncoiled from under a rock and sent her running for cover. No more. She'd run enough. They'd both said it. Trust. Patience.

She stood on tiptoes and kissed him back.

His smile warmed her. "Have a seat." She motioned toward the chair where they'd had their last talk. "How are things with you?"

His smile waned as he pulled out a chair and sat. "I have news."

Her body straightened. "Good or bad?"

He shook his head. "The insurance wasn't approved."

"It wasn't? Oh, Ross, what will you do?"

"Dr. Timmons said he'd resubmit and give them more information. He reminded me that they often reject the first time but approve the next. I'll have to wait and see."

"I assume he knows what he's talking about."

A faint smile returned. "We'll see."

She chuckled. "Silly."

Ross gazed around and then lifted her hand to his lips and kissed it. "How's it feel to have a quiet house again?"

"Good. I love my sister, but…you know how it is…sometimes I could wring her neck."

He nodded. "That's why I stayed away as much as I could. It seemed safer."

She understood his feelings. Moments had arisen when she wished she could have stayed away, too, but sisters try to deal with it. "She did apologize."

He drew back. "Really?" His eyebrows arched. "Tell me."

Her apology was feeble but she'd given it, and Kelsey was at least content that Audrey realized she'd overstepped her bounds. "Audrey admitted that you were a nice man, but she worried about our situations. She admitted that she had been a bit hasty to make a judgment."

Ross drew a slash mark in the air with his finger. "One point for Audrey. At least she made an attempt to undo the damage."

"They left yesterday, and things were amiable. That's important. Jeff didn't say much except once when we were alone. He said you seemed like a nice guy."

He shrugged. "If he only knew."

She gave him a swat. "You're wonderful."

He gave her a wink. "Anyway, I had a talk with Peyton."

"You did?"

"First, I asked her about Lucy and her skating. She said Lucy said she wanted to skate with her since she was new at it." He grinned. "I could tell it made Peyton happy."

Her mouth dry, Kelsey lifted the water glass and took a drink. "They're getting there."

"But she wasn't so happy when I talked about how well she's doing now, and I mentioned that it was time to trade bedrooms."

Being zapped by electricity couldn't have surprised Kelsey more. "You told her that? How did she take it?"

"A bit of drama, but I reminded her that being healthy was far more precious than a bedroom a few feet larger than hers." He wove his fingers through her hand. "I've missed my room and to be honest, I've been resentful at times. Not fair to her. It was my choice, but I know it was a mistake. The guest room I'm using is fine for her."

She lifted their joined hands and kissed his. "I know that was difficult."

"It's for the best. I feel it in here." He pressed his free hand to his chest. "Things will work out with the new medication. I'm confident."

Confident. Kelsey longed to feel that kind of self-assurance.

Ross eyed his watch. "I suppose I should be going." He stood and wrapped his arm around her, then lowered his lips to hers.

As always, her heart soared with her delight. "Call me, and we can—"

The telephone rang. She held up a finger and strode to the phone. Karen. A chill ran down her back. "It's Karen."

His expression sank to concern, and he moved closer.

She lifted the headset her heart in her throat. "Karen, how is—"

The jolt of her response overtook her. She covered the mouthpiece. "Doug's gone. He died this morning."

Chapter Fourteen

When Kelsey hung up, tears rolled from her eyes. It surprised Ross before reality rushed through him. No matter what had happened in the past, Doug had once been her husband, and he was still Lucy's father.

He drew her into his arms, allowing her tears to flow in silence. Her wet grief soaked into his shirt, but he held her closer, kissing her hair and soothing her back with his palm. Too many things had struck Kelsey at once. The fear of Lucy's diagnosis the following Monday and now the death of Lucy's father.

Weight bore down on Ross's shoulders. Finally he had some positive things happening in his life. Despite the insurance issue, a new medication might allow Peyton a normal life—almost normal—but whichever it might be, the outcome would be better than he feared. God willing, Peyton's future seemed brighter. She would become a young woman, date, fall in love, marry and have a child of her own. His heart swelled with the abiding sense that the Lord looked down on him with a smile.

But today grief came again to the woman who'd become a part of him.

A final sob lingered against his chest. He waited. A shudder and deep breath touched his own heart, and he swallowed. "Can I do anything?"

"What you're doing now." She lifted her red eyes to him. "You know that my love for Doug died long ago, but he's Lucy's father, and…"

"Grief is natural, Kelsey. Don't apologize. You have Lucy to face and memories to handle. It's difficult." His wife's death shook him to the core. Telling Peyton she'd died had been one of the most difficult experiences in his life. Tears had rolled down her face while he held her, unable to release his grief because of her. He stayed strong and, once he was alone, he sobbed.

Kelsey eased back, still using his arm for support. "The funeral is Saturday. We'll drive to Grand Rapids on Friday for the viewing and come back Saturday after the funeral."

"Let me take you. You shouldn't drive."

She shook her head and pressed her palm to his cheek. "Thank you so much, but I need to do this alone. Just Lucy and me."

He studied her face. Her steady gaze reflected confidence. "If you change your mind, I'll be happy to go with you. I can find things to do. It's no problem."

Kelsey tilted her head and touched her lips to his in a fleeting kiss. "If I decide I don't want to drive, I promise I'll let you know." She rubbed her temples and shifted backward, her movement unsteady.

Ross stayed beside her until she settled back into the easy chair. Her face changed, and her look concerned him, a kind of anguish so deep it chilled him. "What is it?"

"Me. I'm ashamed. So filled with remorse. I knew he was very sick, Ross, but I didn't make an effort to speak to him. I let my bitterness stop me from doing what God would have me do."

"Kelsey, he hurt you deeply."

"But you said yourself, God didn't ask me to forget. He

asked me to forgive." Tears rimmed her eyes. "Now it's too late."

He rose and knelt at her feet as he drew her hands into his. "No. It's not too late. Karen is still alive, and she needs your support. You have another chance."

She pressed her lips together, a tremor quivering in her cheek. "Another chance." Her voice was but a whisper.

"You can do it, Kelsey." Ross drew her into his arms and held her close, witnessing the tension and confusion that roiled inside her. "If you remember the days of your friendship, when you'd do anything for her, and if you see her betrayal as her failure to fight off temptation, then you can dig deep in your heart and forgive." He captured her gaze. "This has to be more than words. Forgiveness comes from the heart."

Her back stiffened a moment and then her shoulders drooped as her eyes closed. "I know. That's the hard part, Ross. I might be able to say it, but do I mean it?"

Ross didn't try to answer her question. It was one she had to answer herself, but he believed she could if she remembered how forgiven she and all God's children have been by His mercy.

She rose and rested her cheek against his shoulder, her arms holding him close, and they stood in the silence, each with their own thoughts. He remained silent, and then he heard her soft voice shudder the three difficult words. "From the heart."

Kelsey gripped the steering wheel. The day had been long, and Lucy's tears twisted her heart so tightly she could barely breathe. She glanced at her daughter, strapped in beside her, her head nodding in exhausted sleep. Facing Karen had torn her to bits, but standing beside Doug's coffin draped with a Dear Husband bouquet had rendered her nearly helpless.

She'd contained her tears until she escaped to the restroom, where she released the flood of memories and pain for Lucy.

He had aged, gaunt and pale even with the assistance of the funeral home, the strain of death clearly visible on his face. A bolt of regret raced through her. Regret that she hadn't shown more compassion to Karen, and deep regret that she hadn't spoken to Doug when she brought Lucy for a visit. Such a small gesture, yet it might have let him know that her life had moved forward. She was fine. Her love for him had died years earlier.

The lights of the motel signaled her to turn into the entrance driveway. She rolled around to the side and parked, then sat a moment gazing at Lucy, no longer her little girl but almost a teenager. A new wave of pain rolled over her. Monday they would face the specialist and hear the report. Lucy's new problem overwhelmed her. They'd lived with a tentative kind of confidence, but one that grew surer every day. But now her confidence had fluttered away like dry leaves.

Ross swept into her mind, brushing away her darker thoughts. She could count on him. The more she pondered the situation, the more she knew she'd made a great mistake listening to others and taking what they said to heart. Her heart counted more…and Ross's heart, too. Real love stood strong in times of desperation and trials, no matter what conflicts lay in its path. How often had she thought the same thing after Doug had walked out. If their love had been strong, nothing could have pulled him away from his devotion to his wife and daughter.

Real love. Now to face whether what she felt for Ross was real or something else. She'd experienced the emotion of love in his arms and the joy of partnership in their good times and bad. She longed to be with him even now, to feel his arms around her, supporting her and making her feel cherished. To Kelsey, that felt like real love.

Shaking her head, Kelsey ignored her thoughts. She pulled the car keys from the ignition. A room waited for her.

"Lucy." She laid her hand on Lucy's arm.

She opened her eyes, a glazed look curtaining her face before she jerked upward and blinked. "I fell asleep."

"You did, but that's okay. It's been a difficult day for you… for us."

Lucy's lids lowered and opened. "I wish Daddy hadn't died."

"So do I." A chill ran down her arms. She meant what she'd said. That would have given her time to forgive him and might have opened a door for Doug to be a better father to Lucy. Regret. Regret. The emotion belonged to the past. The past was over and gone. Now she faced the future and regret should be replaced with wiser decisions and better choices.

She opened the door and slipped from her sedan. Lucy followed. Kelsey hit the lock button and pulled her room key from her pocket. She slipped it into the outside door's lock and it clicked open. She beckoned Lucy to go in first. The room was a short distance down the hallway, and when she turned on the light, loneliness overcame her.

Tonight Karen would go home and crawl into an empty bed, knowing Doug would never be back to keep her warm. Kelsey had experienced that same sadness once. Yet tonight instead of the bitterness she'd clung to for so long, sorrow had washed it away. She grieved for Karen and Lucy's loss.

Kelsey looked up as Lucy carried her pajamas into the bathroom. In moments, the shower sounded, and Kelsey settled into the only easy chair and closed her eyes. She dreaded tomorrow. Because Doug and Karen had no church connection, the funeral would be held at the funeral home. Doug's father and sister had come for the funeral, and she'd spoken to them, but it had been years. She'd been sad to learn that Doug's mother had died from cancer three years ago. Doug had never told her. Or maybe she hadn't listened. The weight of that possibility dragged her back into a dark place.

Grateful when the shower stopped, Kelsey rose and pulled out her nightgown. She refused to wallow in her bad choices and mistakes. She'd blamed Doug so long that she'd overlooked her own part in undoing any hope for a relationship after their divorce. *Divorce* had been a word she'd learned to dismiss. It wouldn't happen to her, a Christian. But it had and, unknowingly, she'd remained faithful to a dead marriage.

Today she would be free from the bonds of her oath to Doug, but the thought gave her no pleasure. Instead, she'd faced what she had to do. Now she needed to figure out how.

Lucy came out from her shower with rosy cheeks and climbed into bed. She fell asleep before Kelsey had slipped into the bathroom.

Kelsey didn't linger in the shower. She greeted the bed, snapped off the light and slid under the covers, her prayers rising for answers and for a night of rest.

At the funeral luncheon, Doug's father and sister chose seats across from Lucy, and though Kelsey felt uncomfortable, she accepted the situation. They seemed to know a few people there, and he was Lucy's grandfather and she, Lucy's aunt. They'd talked about a few things, and she found that neither one harbored any grudges. In fact, Doug's father apologized for his son's actions. Over the years, he had never offered any solace or comment on the breakup of her and Doug's marriage, and the only attention he and his wife had paid to Lucy was an occasional card with a check. Doug's parents apparently focused on his sister's children, who were nearby and didn't remind them of Doug's behavior. She sensed, too, that they didn't know how to deal with Lucy's illness. Though she'd resented their avoidance for years, those feelings had fallen by the wayside when she had more trying situations to face.

Guests stopped by periodically to give their condolences to Lucy, and they also spoke to her. As time passed, Kelsey found it easier to accept their sympathy and made a point to show Lucy how many people loved her father.

Distracted, Kelsey didn't notice Karen at her side until she spoke. "I hope you'll stick around before leaving for home." Tension etched her face. Her former friend had not only lost her husband but now had to face the friend she'd betrayed.

"Well, I'd planned to—"

"I have a few items I'd like to give Lucy that belonged to her dad. You know, so she remembers."

Her voice caught, and sorrow knotted in Kelsey's throat. She'd been unable to speak with Karen alone with so many mourners around. Even last night, visitors stayed and offered to take her out to eat. It left no time for them to talk, but this invitation opened the door that Kelsey dreaded, yet knew the Lord wanted her to step inside. "I'll wait as long as I can. We have a three-hour drive home."

"I know." She scanned the tables at the lovely restaurant she'd chosen. "See." She made a fleeting gesture toward them. "Many people are leaving. It shouldn't be long."

Kelsey gazed at Lucy, her eyes shifting from her to Karen as she listened. "Would you like to see what Karen has for you?"

She nodded. "She's giving me some of Daddy's things."

"That's nice, isn't it?"

Relief touched Karen's face, and she walked away to say goodbye to those ready to leave.

Lucy dug into the dessert that she'd only played with—very unusual for her. But Kelsey leaned back with no interest in her dessert or the food they'd served. Her stomach had been churning all morning. The funeral broke her heart. Doug had not been an active Christian, but he'd occasionally attended church, and she considered him a believer. Sitting at his funeral and hearing references that he'd gone to a better place and he'd remain as the wind in the trees tore her in two. What about heaven and everlasting life? Where had that been in this funeral empty of hope and with nothing to provide Karen with a sense of peace and comfort?

Her cheek ticked with the anguish she felt. Kelsey wanted to remind Karen of the solace she could find laying her burdens at Jesus's feet. The thoughts hurt too much, and she forced her mind to let it drop for now. But instead, her thoughts of faith reminded her that she'd come to offer forgiveness, and she'd yet to be confident that it came, as Ross had said, from the heart.

After breakfast before they had left for the funeral, she'd opened the Gideon's Bible she found in a dresser drawer. As she scanned the pages in the Gospel books, the theme of forgiveness jumped from the pages. Every verse reminded her that if she forgave, the Lord would forgive her, but she didn't want forgiveness because she was afraid of not being forgiven. She knew the Lord had forgiven her sins. It was His promise. Yet her own peace of mind, her own expression of faith knew that forgiveness was expected of Christians. Forgive your enemies. She'd read that a multitude of times.

She came to the last book of the Gospels, and her eyes grazed the pages until she came to Luke 6:37. "Do not judge, and you will not be judged. Do not condemn, and you will not be condemned. Forgive, and you will be forgiven."

Her chest constricted. She'd judged Karen and Doug over and over again. She'd condemned them. She'd held the bitterness like a treasure. Bitterness, like regret, lived in the past. Discarding it meant looking to the future, and that's what she wanted to do.

A noise interrupted her thoughts. Doug's father had risen to say goodbye. He kissed Lucy's cheek and held Kelsey's hand. The distance she'd felt vanished. She hugged him and told him Lucy would welcome his visit.

He smiled at her for the first time. "I'll be in touch. Her birthday is in May."

It was more a question, but he had it right. "Last week. May 20."

"You're almost eleven now, your mom said. Your grandmother would have been proud of you, Lucy."

She smiled and hugged him.

Pride filled Kelsey's chest, watching Lucy make the old man happy, though she barely knew him.

Doug's sister and he waved goodbye and, in moments, the last of Karen's friends had left and they were face-to-face again. Karen lifted her handbag. "Do you know how to get to the house from here?"

"I think so, but I'll follow you just to make sure."

In the car, Lucy turned on the radio and found a station with popular music while Kelsey reviewed her thoughts, wondering what she would say when she arrived, but a calm had settled over her, and she felt the Lord's leading.

The drive was short. She gazed at the house she'd looked at only a few times before, and today it looked forlorn, though it hadn't changed except for Doug's absence. Karen beckoned her inside, and she encouraged Lucy to go first. Once there, she found a seat in the living room while Lucy joined Karen upstairs. She stayed behind, giving them time together. Karen had always loved Lucy before the bad times happened, and seeing them together reminded Kelsey of that.

When they returned, Lucy carried an armload of mementos. She placed them on the sofa and sat beside them.

"Mom, do you want to see what Karen gave me?"

Kelsey's pulse jogged as she settled on the sofa beside the gifts. At a glance, she spotted photographs, a lapel pin of some kind and a small jewelry box.

"What's the pin?" She gazed at the trinket.

"Karen said Daddy won an award for his work with a charity."

Charity. She'd never known him to do much for anyone but his family. She studied the pin.

"He did charity work for the cancer foundation after his mother died." Karen answered her unasked question.

Kelsey looked up, trying to keep the shock from her face. "That's very touching." And it was. Touched her more than she could imagine.

Karen moved closer. "If there's anything you'd like, Kelsey, please let me know. I realize you—"

"No, these things for Lucy are lovely. I don't expect anything."

She laid her hand on Kelsey's arm. "He left some money in his will for Lucy. The attorney will take care of that."

Money. She'd never considered money from Doug. She couldn't control her frown.

"He wanted to help Lucy with college, but now you may need it for…" She paused, her gaze shifting from Lucy back to Kelsey. "You know for her health issues."

"College is a good choice. We have health insurance that's been pretty good."

"I'm glad. Doug worried about that sometimes."

Her expression plunged into Kelsey's heart. Doug worried. She'd learned so much, and she'd closed her mind and feelings off for so long. Today was meant for honesty. "I had no idea, Karen."

"I know. He kept it to himself most of the time."

Lucy opened the velvet box and inside lay a lovely diamond ring. Confused, she peered at Karen.

"It was his mother's. He was saving it for Lucy."

His mother's ring. Tears brimmed in Kelsey's eyes. "The ring is a precious gift. We'll take good care of it."

"I know you will." Karen drew back and stood closer to Lucy.

"Want to see the pictures?" Lucy held the stack of photographs.

"Why don't you take them in the dining room so you have more room to study them, and I'll come in a few minutes." Kelsey hoped Lucy would take her suggestion, giving her time to speak with Karen.

Without a word, Lucy held the photographs close to her chest and headed for the dining room. Knowing the time was now, Kelsey's heart pummeled against her chest. With Lucy out of earshot, she faced Karen. "I want to say a few things before Lucy returns."

Karen drew back, concern growing on her face. "If you're upset with—"

"No, please. You've been thoughtful. You and Doug. I want to ask your forgiveness, Karen."

"My forgiveness?" Her eyes widened, her jaw slack. "I should ask yours."

"No. You hurt me…you and Doug…but I compounded the hurt by my bitterness. I should have encouraged Doug's visits with Lucy. When the worst ache faded, I should have let you know. We could have talked, but I clung to the anger and resentment, even when I no longer cared. It wasn't right and it wasn't the moral thing to do. I know what the Lord expects, and I ignored it."

"But—"

"Forgetting will never happen. You know that. You and I will never be good friends again, but I care about you, Karen. I always have, and I pray that you truly believe what I'm saying. Right now, I'm grieving with you, because you lost a husband. And I grieve that I didn't talk to him when I was here. I didn't let him know that I forgave him, too."

Karen dropped her face in her hands, and Kelsey opened her arms and drew her in. "I know you care about Lucy, and if you want to pick her up for a weekend once in a while, just let me know." Lucy's latest problem filtered through her mind, and when Karen lifted her head and embraced her, Kelsey told her about Lucy's latest diagnosis. "I'll know Monday, and I'll call you."

Tears rolled down Karen's cheeks, and Kelsey held her. She knew soon Lucy would call her to look at the photos, but at the moment, she couldn't leave Karen. And for the first time, she knew the forgiveness she offered was truly from the heart.

Chapter Fifteen

Ross eyed his watch and stared down the road. Kelsey had called and estimated her arrival time, but he didn't want to wait at home. Sitting in front of her house seemed easier than pacing and wearing out his carpet.

She'd said little about the funeral since Lucy was with her, but his mind never left her situation. He knew it would be difficult to deal with the funeral, and he prayed that she'd talked with Karen. The guilt would be lifted from her, and that would be a blessing.

He checked his watch again. A half hour had passed, and he suspected that she would arrive any minute. He leaned back a moment, pondering his news but not wanting to say a word until they talked about her trip.

When he lifted his head, his pulse raced. Kelsey's car was coming down the street, and when she pulled into her driveway, she gave him a questioning look. Alone. A frown pulled at his face.

He stepped from his minivan and hit the lock button on his remote as he approached her car. "How are you? Where's Lucy?"

"She's fine, but she's been so wound up, I called Lexie and

let her go over to see Cooper. He's doing so well now, and I can only hope Lucy's tests will offer the same good news."

Although he loved seeing Lucy, having her busy for a while relieved him. Now they could talk without her listening. He wanted to know so many things.

She opened the rear door and pulled out her overnight case. He looked for the other bag. "Where's Lucy's bag?"

"She took it into Lexie's. She had a couple of things and some photographs from Karen that were Doug's, and she wanted to show Cooper."

Ross took the bag from Kelsey's hands. "Were the gifts okay with you?"

She nodded. "I was happy for Lucy. She needed the connection and the closure."

"I'm glad then." He slipped his hand into hers, and it felt so natural. "I missed you."

She chuckled. "You mean that old saying about absence making the heart grow fonder is true?"

"Undoubtedly." He squeezed her hand as they climbed the few steps to the covered porch. He stood back while she unlocked the door, and she held it open as he carried in her bag. Instead of asking, he headed for the master bedroom and placed it on her bed.

When he returned, he heard Kelsey in the kitchen. "I'm making coffee."

"Perfect." He strode into the room and slipped onto a stool at the island. "How'd it go?"

She drew in a breath and told him the details, but left out what he really wanted to know. "And did you have a chance to talk with Karen?"

She lifted tired eyes to his. "I did. I thought it would be difficult but, you know what? It wasn't. By the time I'd gone through the visitation and the funeral, I ached so badly for her. My feelings for Doug ended so long ago, and though I grieved, it was for Lucy and Karen and for my behavior in not talking with Doug earlier."

He slipped off the stool and moved to her side. "I'm grateful, for your sake." He slid his arm around her back and drew her closer.

"So am I. A heavy weight lifted from me. One I'd carried far too long. I finally realized that bitterness and regret bound me to the past, and I want to look to the future."

His heart sang. "I love hearing you say that." *Love.* The word rippled through his chest. He looked into her eyes, and she responded.

Her mouth drew toward his, and he lowered his lips to hers, drinking in the sweet sense of completeness. He missed her every moment they were apart. She filled his mind each day, and he believed it was possible to be in love and still be focused on two other females he adored—his daughter and Lucy.

Kelsey trembled in his arms, her body yielding against his, the weariness of her trip seeming to melt away. "This feels so right." She tilted her head back and gazed into his eyes. "I thought of you so much while I was gone."

Her face flickered with a new thought. "And ached at a funeral with no faith message. It was so sad. Doug attended church, and I'd always trusted that he was a believer, but the service felt empty and hopeless."

He listened, holding her close and sensing the sorrow she felt. "The Lord knew his heart. That's your hope for him. Shame can pull us from faith, and hopefully in those last days, he returned to what he'd believed." Ross longed for a better answer, one with more assurance, but only the Lord knew the truth. He still had good news to share, and this seemed like the right time. "I heard some good news Friday morning."

She jerked her head upward. "About—?"

"The insurance. The medication is being covered. In fact,

I picked up the prescription right after I heard. Dr. Timmons called it in and Peyton's been on it for two days." His chest expanded with hope.

Her joyful expression sank. "You should have called me."

"I knew you had a lot on your mind, and I didn't want to give you my wonderful news while you were dealing with a difficult situation." His excuse sounded empty. In truth, he wanted to see the happiness on her face. His motivation was selfish.

"Please, tell me all the good news you can. I want to know…and the bad news, too, Ross. If we're this close, we need to share our joys and sorrows."

He nodded as he raised his hand. "Scout's honor. I promise and I'm sorry."

She brushed her lips across his again and eased back. "I smell coffee."

He sniffed the air, smelling the brisk scent, and he grinned.

Kelsey slipped from his arms and headed for the coffeepot, but he prayed that was as far as she would slip away from him. He wanted to hold her forever.

The doctor's voice faded as Kelsey's mind spun with his diagnosis. He gazed at her over his glasses, his face serious, and she knew they had to face his conclusion.

"But…" She shook her head, digging into her thoughts for alternatives. "I don't understand. What about gamma knife surgery?" It was noninvasive and safer, with only a short hospital stay, but Dr. Bryant only looked at her, his eyes intense.

"I just explained that, Mrs. Rhodes."

She flinched, wondering where her mind had been when he'd told her. She lowered her head. "I'm sorry." Her hands twisted in her lap, and she couldn't bear to look at Lucy.

"We're still not sure until we get inside if it's an actual tumor or scar tissue, and the gamma knife can lead to more scar tissue. We want this surgery to be the final one for Lucy.

If it's not a tumor, then we've won a battle, and the scar tissue can be removed, hopefully for the last time."

"The last time." She spoke the words bursting in her head. "If only we could count on that."

"You've been doing well, right, Lucy?"

"I've been great. No symptoms even."

Kelsey finally turned her head to see her daughter's face. She looked strong and determined to win the battle. "But a craniotomy. Is that our only choice?" That was the word she didn't want to hear. A craniotomy meant opening her skull and removing a bone flap. It meant Lucy would lose her lovely hair again. It meant…too much. She fought her tears.

"It is because it's the best way to remove whatever is growing. We can keep our fingers crossed—pray—that Lucy will be on the road to health again. And it's a small setback if she's tumor free. If not, we've taken care of it before it grows, and that's good, too."

"It's not a tumor." Lucy's voice cut through his final word.

Dr. Bryant blinked. "You sound confident, Lucy."

"I am, because I prayed." Her jaw had set in determination.

He gave a desperate look at Kelsey. "That's very good, but do you realize that…"

Kelsey jumped to his assistance. "Lucy knows that sometimes God's answer is no. She's still confident."

He flipped her file closed. "Okay, then." He drew in a deep breath. "That is how it stands. We'll need to set a surgery date. I'll schedule you for some lab tests, and you'll donate some blood. Don't take any aspirin or medication that might thin the blood. Okay? You both know the routine."

Too well. Kelsey rose and stepped toward the doorway while Lucy unfolded her body from the chair and followed. She said goodbye, then draped her arm across Lucy's shoulders. As she did, Lucy's blond curls brushed her arm and her heart ached. She swallowed her tears and managed to suppress her emotions.

When they reached the car, Lucy tilted her head upward, searching her mother's eyes. And as Kelsey grasped the door handle, Lucy patted her hand. "It's okay, Mom."

Kelsey's chest compressed. "I know it will be, sweetie." The endearment gave her away.

Lucy gave a final pat and rounded the car to the passenger side. "Can we stop at Peyton's house?"

Kelsey drew back at Lucy's question. "Why do you want to go there?"

"Because they care about me, and you'll want to talk with Ross." Pure innocence shown on her face.

"I planned to call him." She glanced at her watch. "We can drive by, and if they're home, we'll stop."

Lucy gave a nod and leaned back, listening to the music she'd turned on earlier. The upbeat music resounded in a heavy bass thump-thump, capturing the rhythm of Kelsey's heart. Lucy's request had come out of nowhere. The girls' relationship had yet to stabilize—friendly one day and distant the next, but today could bring a giant leap toward solidifying their friendship.

When the car rolled down Ross's street, she saw his minivan in the driveway. She needed Ross's strength right now. Yet the same dread rippled down her spine. Two girls struggling between life and death. Yet neither had bonded with the other. Two parents who had connected but who struggled with their daughters' health issues and too little time to give to each other. Would the fear ever end? Awash in hopelessness, she pulled in and parked, sending up a prayer for the Lord to take charge. Everything was out of her hands.

Lucy jumped out, hurried toward the front door and rang the bell before Kelsey reached the steps. When the door opened, Ross's eyes widened in concern. "Lucy, what's—"

Then he spotted her coming up the sidewalk and looked relieved. "This is a nice surprise." But as he said the words, his expression changed. "You're coming from the doctor's appointment, aren't you?"

Kelsey nodded. "Lucy asked to stop by. I hope it's okay."

"Okay?" He slipped his arm around her shoulders. "It's where you should be."

His words rushed through her. In his face, she saw that his words had a deeper meaning. Her chest throbbed. "Can we talk?"

Worry spread over his face as he steered her into the great room. "Peyton's in her bedroom, Lucy." He motioned toward the doorway.

Lucy rapped on the door and slipped inside as Ross drew Kelsey into his arms. "Bad news?"

She nodded, fearing she would break into a sob. "We've been through this before, Ross, but this time I don't think I can handle it. It's been too much. Too much emotion with Doug's death. Too much vacillating about our relationship. I'm bouncing off walls with no way to stop."

He cradled her head and pressed it to his shoulders. Though he was silent, his action spoke clearly. The tears she'd held back streamed from her eyes onto his knit shirt. His firm hand massaged her back while the other held her tightly. His breathing eased his own tension, giving hers direction to follow. She drew in a ragged breath, and released it into acceptance.

"I'm glad you came." Ross's whisper brushed her cheek. "You belong here with me to share the worry and disappointment." He eased back and longing filled his eyes. "Let's sit and you can tell me what happened."

She shifted to the sofa, his arm still supporting her, and she sank into the cushion. The specialist's report tumbled from her as she wrestled with her sagging emotions, but

Ross's firm touch, the compassion lighting his face, gave her courage.

"The surgery is bad news, but you still have a lot to pray about. Scar tissue is better than another tumor. At this point, they aren't sure. So let's think positive."

"I'm trying." His words inched a grin to her lips. "You should have heard Lucy."

"Did she cry?" He looked confused.

"No, she told the doctor it was nothing, because she'd prayed."

A whoosh of air escaped his lips. "What a girl. And you know what? She's right. Children have enough faith to let the Lord move mountains. She knows her body, and she understands her physical symptoms. Lucy could be right."

The explanation sizzled through Kelsey. She hadn't thought of that, and the idea renewed her hope. "That's true. So I need to—"

Peyton's door flew open, and the girls charged into the room. "Dad, Lucy's head has to be opened up."

Kelsey rose, seeing how distraught she was. She hurried to her and pulled Peyton into her arms. "It sounds terrible, Peyton, but Lucy's been through this before, and she'll be fine again."

Peyton's eyes searched hers, then turned to her dad. "But they shave her head and put a big hole in her skull."

Kelsey couldn't talk around that. It was too true. She wished Lucy hadn't been so graphic. "Her hair grows back, and the hole will be repaired." It sounded so mechanical. So simplified. She was at a loss for the right words.

Lucy edged closer and wriggled her way into the embrace. "I'll be fine, Peyton. I promise."

Peyton drew back and wrapped her arms around Lucy. "I'll pray for you every day."

Kelsey shifted toward Ross, witnessing the amazing bonding she and Ross had hoped for. But today it faded in light of the thoughts that had just rushed through her mind. This would be their lives—if not one daughter, then the other. No relationship could survive the constant stress.

Ross's mouth stood agape as he observed the girls. He pulled his gaze away and looked at her. "Another prayer answered." He slipped to her side and slid his arm around her back.

Kelsey stood in his embrace, cherishing the moment. With God all things were possible, and she would try to cling to that truth, even though everything felt hopeless.

Kelsey watched through the window and saw Ross standing at the door while Peyton rolled her overnight case up the walk. That was a first. Usually Ross didn't let Peyton carry a thing. Kelsey stepped from the dining room into the foyer and pulled open the door as Peyton's case bounced up the low steps to the porch. Ross stood back as she rolled it inside.

"Peyton." She gave her a one-armed hug. "You can take your luggage into Lucy's bedroom."

Peyton turned down the hallway.

When she vanished, Kelsey faced Ross. "If she and Lucy want to share the room, that's fine, or Lucy is willing to sleep upstairs if Peyton wants a room of her own."

"She's never spent the night with any girlfriend. I think she'll want to have a real pajama party." He studied her face, but she was unable to control her grin. "If that's what they still call it."

"I do, but the girls call it an overnighter." She chuckled at his lack of knowledge.

He grinned back. "Thanks so much for this. You're sure you won't mind? I'm not inconveniencing you?"

"I'm glad to have her here. It's a good distraction for Lucy. She's off all her medication that could be a problem during surgery, and now it's just wait. You know what that means."

From his expression, he understood. "And she'll still have labwork."

She nodded. "Probably a day or two before the surgery."

"Which is coming up too fast."

His comment jarred her, yet it was true. "But it will be wonderful to get it over with."

He gave her a thumbs-up. "And to hear the good news."

She realized that his action stemmed from the concern she couldn't hide. Good news had been her prayer since she'd heard that Lucy needed to undergo yet another surgery.

He checked his watch and sidled closer. "I hope Peyton's okay spending the night."

Typical parent. Kelsey chuckled. "Don't worry. She'll be fine. Anyway, we have plans that'll keep them both busy. And really, don't rush. Pick her up anytime tomorrow."

"Thanks." His expression changed. "Today Ethan suggested I arrange a Dreams Come True trip for Peyton, but I—"

"That's a great idea, Ross. She's been sick so long."

"But it wouldn't be right now."

"Right?" Her mind spun. "Why?" He made no sense.

He touched her cheek. "Not with Lucy's problems again. The girls have finally gotten closer. A Dreams Come True trip for Peyton could be their undoing."

"Ross, no. She deserves—"

"No. Lucy deserves it, too, and now she can't."

Her emotions spun out of control. His comment proved what her heart told her. They couldn't spend their lives stopping one daughter from enjoying life because the other was ill. That's what their relationship would be. That's all it could be.

"Really, it's for the best. Maybe another time." He glanced at his watch again. "I'd better be on my way. I'm picking up Ethan and he expected me fifteen minutes ago." He grinned. "Two guys out on the town."

"Right." She gave him a playful swat, realizing that he was trying to lift her spirit.

Then Kelsey saw it coming. Ross lowered his lips and gave her a quick kiss. When he drew back, she glanced around him. The girls had never observed affection, and she didn't want to confuse them. And she didn't want to confuse herself.

"Drive carefully." But as she looked into his eyes, her wavering heart gave another kick. Being close to someone who cared about her felt so good. She tilted her head and pressed her lips to his again, but this time they lingered. Her heart took flight as it did when he touched her, and when he left, the same loneliness would seep into her chest until she saw him again. The growing sensation rioted inside her. What was she doing?

Ross headed to the car, and when he turned around, she wiggled her fingers in a goodbye wave, her heart tripping again. Goodbye. Could she ever say it and mean it? Goodbye forever? She watched his car vanish, headed back to the living room, but as she passed the hallway, Lucy's door opened, and the girls peeked out.

"Is he gone?" Lucy glanced toward Peyton leaning over her shoulder.

"Peyton, he didn't say goodbye again, because—"

"That's okay." Peyton's smile brightened. "We said goodbye, but I'm anxious to start the Father's Day present."

Kelsey's tension lessened, seeing the excitement on Peyton's face. "The present. Great." She drew closer to Lucy's room. "Did you find some photographs like the ones I mentioned?"

Lucy flung the door open and Kelsey saw photographs spread out on her bed. "Wow! That's a lot of pictures." She'd only purchased one scrapbook.

"Mom, she brought lots so we can pick the best." Lucy's eyes rolled, as they so often did.

"Okay. That was smart." She wandered into the room and gazed at the photos. Her heart knotted when she saw Ross's wedding photo with Ruthie, photos of them with Peyton as a baby and as a toddler. "How did you find these?" Her expression looked like a conspirator's.

"Dad didn't move everything out of the bedroom when I moved in. Those built-in shelves that have doors on them are filled with old albums that my mom kept there. I think he forgot, but I used to look at them after my mom died so I wouldn't forget her."

Kelsey grasped a photo and gazed at it, pressing her lips together to hold back her sob. She'd been about six when her own mother died. Picturing Peyton stealing away to look at these photos broke her heart. Managing to hold back her tears, she placed the photograph back with the others and drew Peyton into her arms. "That was a good thing to do, Peyton, but I don't think you'd ever forget your mom, even though you were young."

"I won't." Her embrace tightened, and Kelsey struggled again to waylay her emotion.

"Okay." She eased back and motioned to the photos. "Pick out about twenty of your favorites and if we have room, we can add some more."

Peyton nodded as she eyed the spread of snapshots. "But—" She swung around. "I don't have any of you and Lucy. I want some of those, too."

Kelsey's pulse skittered. "Are you sure?"

Peyton's eyes widened. "You're like a mom to me, and Lucy's like my sister. You should be in the scrapbook, too."

Peyton undid her. She pulled the girl into her arms and kissed her hair, holding her close. Her cheek quaked with emotion, and she grabbed a breath before she tried to speak. "Thank you, Peyton." The love in the girl's eyes struck her like a blow. Saying goodbye to Ross meant walking out on Peyton. Kelsey's wounds deepened.

Lucy looked on, her eyes shifting from her to Peyton, and Kelsey wasn't sure how she felt about the girl's declaration, but in moments, she wrapped her arm around Peyton. "You are just like a new sister."

Kelsey willed herself to straighten. Her legs trembled as she moved toward the door. "Here's what we'll do. While you start on the scrapbook, Lucy can go through a few of our photos. We have some nice ones from Lucy's birthday party." The silly photo of Ross and her balancing on one foot to please Audrey came to mind. She wouldn't call that one nice. It was ridiculous, but it was fun.

A few minutes later, the two girls sat at the dining-room table covered in newspaper while they sorted photos and looked at the scrapbooking supplies she'd purchased. "You know how to do this, right?"

Peyton shuffled through the background sheets she'd bought. "I saw a TV program about scrapbooking so I know a little." She looked up. "But if I have a problem, I'll let you know."

Kelsey pulled out some of the decorative accessories. "Here you have these little bubbles where you can add words and make it look like they're talking—like in a cartoon. And these are different things to make the page fun." She gave them a few stickers and die cuts. "I'm going into the kitchen, and if you need me just holler."

Both girls were already delving into the supplies before she finished speaking. She shrugged and slipped through the doorway. In the kitchen, she started making cookies, forcing herself to forget her depressing concerns. In the background, the girls' voices jumbled together in conversation, although she couldn't make out their words.

The scent of cookies filled the air when she pulled them from the oven. As if she'd rung a fire alarm, Lucy and Peyton charged into the room, sniffing the air. She poured each one a glass of milk and set out a small plate of warm cookies.

They slipped onto stools at the island and watched her make another batch.

"Mom."

Kelsey turned and waited.

Lucy's eyes shifted as if she were uncertain what to say.

"Is something wrong?"

"No, but I want to know when I'm going to start getting curves like Peyton."

Peyton gave her a poke.

The question caught her off guard, and Kelsey stood a second without knowing what to say. She licked her lips. "Peyton's a year older, so you'll get more curves in another year." She pointed to Lucy's slender waist. "See, you have curves starting already."

She gazed at herself a moment before raising her head. "The day school let out, a boy flirted with Peyton. He told her he'd miss her during the summer."

"You weren't supposed to say anything, Lucy." Peyton jammed her fists into her waist. "I'm not going to tell you anything again."

Lucy's eyes widened. "But this is my mom. I thought you meant not to tell your dad."

Peyton huffed while Kelsey got her bearings. So this was the problem. Boys. Her mind spun. "Maybe the boy just wants to be a friend, Peyton. They're not always flirting."

She looked down at her lap. "He told me I was pretty."

Pretty. Kelsey swallowed. "That's a nice compliment. Do you think he's handsome?"

"Sort of."

"See. He did more than think it. He told you." She bit her lip. Yes, she was a mother, but she was new at this. Inadequate. "Your dad would know more about how boys think." She pictured Ross wanting to chase the boys away with a shovel. The image made her grin.

"I heard girls talking in class about things, but I don't think Dad knows about them or else he doesn't want to tell me."

A knot formed in her stomach. "It's hard for a father to talk with his daughter about personal things and the changes she goes through."

"But who'll tell me so I know it's right?" Peyton's eyes searched hers.

Kelsey grasped her wavering common sense. She pulled up a stool and grabbed a cookie. Anything to delay her response. Her mind worked overtime until she'd organized her thoughts. "Would you like me to explain some things to you, Peyton?"

She nodded, a grateful look spread across her face.

"Mom, what about me?"

"You're old enough, too, Lucy." She drew in a breath. "I'll explain a few things and then if you have questions I'll try to answer them."

She sent up a quick prayer and began. The girls didn't flinch nor did their eyes waver. They seemed to drink in what she explained, and when her mind had run dry, she paused. "Do you understand?"

They both nodded, but she read Peyton's expression and knew a question was coming. "And that's going to happen to me someday."

"Soon, Peyton. You're growing up fast so don't be afraid when it happens. It's natural."

Lucy leaned forward. "And then she can have babies, right?"

Babies. Kelley's lungs drained. "Yes, God had all this happen so when a woman gets married and has a husband to be the father of the baby, her body will have everything she needs."

A faint frown settled on Lucy's brow. "I can have babies, too, in another year maybe."

"Lucy, the Bible tells us to be chaste until we have a husband who can be the father."

"What's *chaste?*"

Her shoulders slumped. *Chaste.* Another way to phrase it would have been better. She stared at Lucy, her mind tumbling. Get yourself out of this one, Kelsey.

Chapter Sixteen

Ross unwrapped the large box and pulled off the tissue. A photograph of Ruthie at his wedding adorned the cover. His heart surged, and he raised his eyes to Peyton. "You made this?"

She nodded. "Look inside."

Somehow, Peyton had found photographs from the past. Memories coursed through his mind. Peyton as a baby, a toddler, Ruthie reading her a book, her first birthday. She'd decorated it with hearts and baby rattles stickers. He shook his head, amazed that she'd created something so special. "I'll bet you had lots of help on this."

"She didn't."

He gazed at Kelsey, a smile bursting from her face.

"No?" He'd guessed Kelsey had done most of it.

"I found the scrapbooking equipment, and she did it all. Lucy helped with the photos."

"Thank you." He flipped to another page where she had created a tie-shape design with a photograph of Peyton and him in a suit, standing by his old sedan. "Heading for the Easter service here." He tapped the photo.

His heart swelled as he turned pages, watching his life flash past—the Christmas tree with gifts beneath and Peyton trying to snoop, a backyard barbecue, and Ruthie just home following a long stay in the hospital. A "Welcome Home" banner hung from an archway with Peyton's crayoned message.

Another page decorated with flowers took his breath away. Photographs of Lucy and Kelsey scattered across the page, and on the opposite side, he studied the precious shot of Lucy and Peyton skating together at the roller rink, the day things changed. He grinned as he focused on the laughable snapshot of Kelsey and him on roller skates.

The last photograph framed in white and decorated with a cross and a large bridal bouquet decoration showed Kelsey and him standing together in front of the Lexie's fireplace the day of her wedding to Ethan. It seemed long ago when he and Kelsey stood beside them to witness their wedding. He sensed that the Lord had been at work in his life that day.

They'd struggled a long time to make themselves accept God's plan for them. So much seemed to be against the rationale that two people with seriously ill children could find love and contentment together. But they had.

"I love this, Peyton." He rose and wrapped her in his arms as he kissed her forehead. "You did a beautiful job, and Lucy…" He looked over his shoulder so he could see her as she hung over the back of his chair. "Thank you for the photos of you and your mom."

"And you, too, Kelsey, for providing the album and all the decorations." He slipped his arm behind her waist and shook his head. "I'm surrounded by women. You two girls are so grown-up. It seems as if every day—"

"But we aren't old enough to have babies yet." Lucy's voice sent his thoughts scattering. "Peyton will have them before me."

He stared at her, dazed and confused. He sought Kelsey for help.

She looked as startled as he felt.

Peyton slammed her fists into her sides. "Lucy, you weren't supposed to say that."

He eyed Peyton. "She wasn't supposed to say what?"

Kelsey held up her hand. "Girls, why don't you two go into the kitchen and get the cake ready so we can eat. And snap the button on the coffeemaker. It's ready to go." She shooed them away.

Peyton hadn't moved until Lucy gave her one of her looks. "Let's go."

They bustled into the kitchen, and Kelsey sank beside him. "I'm sorry, Ross. I didn't have time to tell you."

His face burned with indignation. "You gave Peyton a talk on womanhood and didn't tell me. Didn't ask me?"

She drew back as if he'd slapped her. "Listen to me, Ross." She glanced toward the kitchen doorway and lowered her voice. "How many times have you told me you wished Ruthie were alive to talk with Peyton? I didn't choose to do this. Lucy asked me a question about Peyton's maturing figure, and one question led to another. Did you want me to lie or be evasive?"

"No, but—" But what? She was right. He'd dreaded the day he had to explain Peyton's maturing body and all the things that were beginning to happen to her. "I—I." He closed his eyes and focused. "I'm just startled. I suppose I wanted time to prepare. What if she asks me questions? I won't know what you told her or how to answer her."

Kelsey rose and stood over him. "Tell her the truth. I'm sorry, Ross. It happened. She wanted to know things, and I didn't want to ignore her or even scare her by not explaining. The girls both accepted it and seemed relieved to understand what they were hearing in school."

"In school." He hadn't thought about that. Some parents were quicker to talk to their kids, and some kids probably learned from street talk. Which would he prefer? "Forgive me." Embarrassed by his reaction, Ross looked into her eyes, hoping she saw his regret. She'd done him a huge favor. "I'm surprised at my response. I wasn't prepared for Peyton to open up to you." Envy. Mortified, he shook his head.

"Please don't apologize." She settled beside him again and touched his arm. "I think I understand. You're her dad, and you missed out on sharing something precious with her. I should have thought about it first, but I was in a spot."

"You did the right thing. I'm being silly."

She leaned closer to his ear. "She won't ask, but you can talk to her about boys."

His pulse skipped. "What about boys?"

"I think one of the boys at school has a crush on her. Just before school let out, the boy told her she was pretty and he'd miss her during the summer."

His back straightened. "Peyton? My Peyton? A boy?"

He looked at her and knew she was trying not to laugh. He didn't think it was funny.

"It wasn't a proposal, Ross. He gave her a compliment."

"But she's only twelve."

Kelsey burst into laughter, and he fell back, hearing his ridiculous comment. "She's twelve, becoming a young woman, and one day…"

"One day, when she's maybe sixteen…?"

He shrugged. "We'll see." He released the air strangling in his lungs. "I suppose I can explain about boys if she wants to know."

"Good. Then my job is done."

His chest constricted as her eyes locked with his, and he drew her closer. "No, it's not. You're just beginning." He pressed his lips to hers, wrapped in her warmth.

"Dad!"

He jerked back and turned to find Peyton and Lucy staring at him, their eyes like full moons. He withdrew his arms from Kelsey, gave her a desperate look, and approached Peyton.

"When you are eighteen, you'll have a boyfriend, and he might kiss you good-night. That's what adults do."

She jammed her fists onto her hips again. "Dad, I know that. I was just surprised. I'm not stupid." A frown grew on her face. "And what do you mean when I'm eighteen?"

"Right." Lucy strolled toward them. "Most girls get to go out with boys when they're sixteen."

Kelsey tittered behind him, and he could barely contain his laughter.

Ross looked at his watch, his other hand holding Kelsey's. "How long does the surgery take?"

She gazed at the clock. "He said three to five hours, and he warned us it could be longer. It's been about three and a half now."

"Then I can stop worrying." He glanced at Peyton, her novel lying on the table and her eyes closed. He watched to see if she were sleeping. "Are you okay?"

She nodded.

Kelsey leaned over and patted her leg. "It's a long day, Peyton. Do you want your dad to take you to the cafeteria?"

She shook her head. "I want to wait in case someone comes."

Kelsey gave him a half grin and returned to her magazine.

He hadn't been able to focus on anything. This kind of procedure was new to him. One wrong move and the brain could be damaged. His throat constricted as he imagined Lucy different than she was now. Her buoyant personality had gotten under his skin, and she might as well be his daughter for the fear he felt.

Before her surgery, Lucy looked so small and helpless, but her bravery astounded him. "I'll be fine. Wait and see." The words rang in his head. If only he had that kind of confidence. He flipped the newspaper over in his lap. Crossword puzzles never interested him, but he'd tried to concentrate on a few words. His mind blanked at every definition. He tossed the paper onto the table beside Peyton and twiddled his thumbs. When that didn't work, he rose and stepped into the hallway. Pacing seemed like the answer.

As he trudged up and down the corridor, Ross forced his mind onto other things, and when he looked and spotted a surgeon heading for the waiting room, mask dangling around his neck, Ross slipped back inside. He caught Kelsey's eye. "I think he's coming." Before he could sit, the surgeon called for Kelsey. Peyton jumped from her seat. He slipped his hand into Kelsey's, and the three of them stepped into the hallway.

"Everything went well, and I know you'll be glad to hear the problem was scar tissue."

"Scar tissue." Kelsey's hand rose to her chest. "Thank You, Lord."

The surgeon smiled. "It's a relief, I know. I'll want to keep an eye on it, since it had grown a little, but there were no signs of any other problems. She's in ICU just as a precautionary measure, but when she awakens, a nurse will come to get you."

Kelsey extended her hand. "Thank you, doctor. I'm so relieved."

He nodded, aware of her worry, and then smiled at Peyton and Ross. "You can take a break now. Visit the cafeteria. You won't be called for at least an hour."

Ross shook the surgeon's hand. "Thanks so much."

He slid his arm around Kelsey's back, and they watched the surgeon retreat, but a sob caught his attention, and he turned to Peyton. Tears rolled down her cheeks. He slipped his arm from Kelsey and drew Peyton into his arms. "Go ahead and cry. I know they're happy tears."

Though she didn't speak, she nodded. Her body quivered with emotion, and his heart filled with gratefulness for her change of heart. He recalled Lucy and Peyton's first meetings and how unsuccessful they were. Now they'd become like sisters. He sent a silent prayer of thankfulness.

Kelsey moved beside them and kissed Peyton's hair. "She'll be as good as new very soon, and we'll see her in a while once she wakes up."

Ross shifted back, still keeping one arm around his daughter. "How about some food? Anyone hungry?"

He chuckled when he heard even Peyton give a rousing yes.

Inside the cafeteria, they moved from station to station, salad here, sandwiches there, burgers and fries across the way, and when they'd filled their trays and paid, he located a table near the window where they could see the sun shining. Beds of colorful flowers added to their happy feelings.

His gaze drifted to Peyton. Her new medication had changed her life. The arrhythmia she'd dealt with for so long had subsided. Since the day she pulled her own luggage into Kelsey's, he gave her no more arguments. If she wanted to do things herself, he allowed it. She needed to learn to live with her damaged heart, and he'd probably coddled her too much, now that he thought about it. Maybe Kelsey wasn't so wrong after all.

Peyton gave him a questioning look. "Why are you looking at me?"

"Because I'm proud of you."

A frown crinkled her smooth forehead. "That's not why."

"I guess it's because I'm so happy that your medicine is helping you. It could change your life." His imagination soared.

"Maybe we could actually go on a vacation, Dad." She gave him a silly smile. "Someplace that's not next to a hospital."

A chuckle burst from Kelsey, and he laughed with her. "I was always afraid to be too far from a town that had a good medical facility."

"We've been through the same thing with Lucy, except not quite so bad. At least her problem gave us more warning."

Hearing Lucy's name, Ross eyed his watch. Another half hour. "Does Lucy have a place she's always wanted to go?"

Kelsey chuckled. "You know my daughter. She read a book about a girl in Paris. She wanted to go there. Then it was Hawaii. In another book, the girl went to New York City. Now she wants to go everywhere."

"Me, too." Peyton's eyes glistened, and Ross loved to see her excitement. "Paris. We could see the Eiffel Tower and ride to the top. Dad?" She wiggled her eyebrows. "It's the city of romance."

Romance. Air drained from Kelsey's lungs. She'd waited too long. Even Peyton had made assumptions about their relationship.

"Peyton." He gave her a playful smack.

She giggled. "How about Hawaii? I could wear flowers in my hair and learn to hula." Her gaze shifted to Kelsey.

Kelsey felt compelled to respond. "Hawaii sounds lovely."

Ross's mind captured the excitement. A honeymoon in Hawaii. He drew in a deep breath and relaxed in a pool of sunny thoughts.

"You know, I should call Audrey, and I promised Karen I'd call her."

Kelsey's voice nudged away his dreams.

She scooted back her chair. "I'll go out in the hallway where it's quiet."

He nodded. "We're almost done here. Go ahead and we'll meet you there."

She scurried away, digging out her cell phone, leaving Ross with romantic images zinging through his mind. He tucked those away and gazed at Peyton across the table. "It's wonderful to see you and Lucy friends."

She lowered her head a moment, then looked at him. "I'm ashamed of how I behaved when we first met. I'd never had a friend since I got sick. Even when I tried to be nice, kids seemed to avoid me, so I decided to ignore them. It hurt me and made me sad."

He slipped his hand over hers and squeezed. "It'll still take some time for the kids to see that you've changed, and you'll always have to be careful. Your arrhythmia will hopefully stay under control, but you still have a heart that needs watching. You know that?"

"I know, Daddy, but not living with that fear of a blood clot and having to take coumadin—that might be over, and I'm so happy." She leaned forward, her eyes locked with his. "And I love Kelsey. She's like a second mom to me, and Lucy's a pain sometimes—especially when she can't keep her mouth closed—but I love her, too. I realized that when she got sick."

Ross's voice hung in his throat. Happiness swelled in his chest, and he gazed at his grown-up little girl, wishing away the tears that pushed behind his eyes. "Do you really mean that about Kelsey?"

"You mean being like a mom?"

He nodded.

A worried look grew on her face. "Is that wrong? I still love Mom, but she's—"

"No. No. It's not wrong. I'm thrilled hearing you say you really care about her, and Mom would be so happy."

She studied his face. "You think so?"

"I know it."

A smile seeped from under her concern. "I'm finally feeling sort of like a family."

He slipped around the table and sat beside her, his arm around her shoulders. "Me, too. A complete family."

Kelsey paced the living room, her attention drawn to every noise she heard outside. The sound of a car caused her to veer for the window. When she looked out, her shoulders slumped, and she rubbed the taut cords in her neck. She'd gone over and over her thoughts a thousand times, and she ended up back at the same place. With God all things were possible, but with her, they weren't.

Another sound alerted her, and when she looked, her lungs failed her. She closed her eyes and bowed her head, not knowing what to pray for but needing guidance. Ross's car door slammed, and she approached the front door. When she touched the knob, ice ran down through her veins. She'd never felt so alone.

Feeling the knob turn, she pulled open the door, but when she tried to speak, her throat constricted. She motioned him inside, and though he faltered, he charged in, then turned to face her. "What's happened?" His hand dragged across his jaw, his eyes fraught with concern. "Please, tell me it's not Lucy."

The lump in her throat swelled as she shook her head. Finally, she grasped her wits. "Have a seat, Ross. This isn't about Lucy. It's about…us."

"Us?" He jerked backward, bewilderment drenching his face. "What do you mean?"

"Please sit. I need to explain." She wanted to clutch him to her to ease his pain. Her own anguish rattled her bones as she sank into the nearest chair.

Ross stood over her, his fists clenched. "Kelsey, have I done something? I thought we—"

"So did I. I wanted everything to be fine, but deep inside, I—I—"

"You have no feelings for me? Or is it Peyton?" His shoulders slumped.

Her heart ached seeing the expression on his face. "No, that's not it. I care. I care about you both." She cared too much. But… "Please sit, and I'll try to make sense out of this."

He crumpled onto the sofa, elbows on his thighs and his head hanging. "Please, make sense." He lifted his gaze to hers. "Since you called, I've been in a daze. I knew something was wrong. Terribly wrong, but I didn't expect this."

She gnawed the edge of her lip, searching for words, thoughts that made sense not long ago, but they'd fluttered away like frightened birds. "Do you remember a while back when you talked about taking Peyton on a Dreams Come True trip and—"

"Yes. I'd love to do that, but I wanted to wait until—"

"Until Lucy was out of danger. I know."

His brows drew together, his eyes narrowing. "I thought that would please you."

"But it didn't. It reminded me of how I made Lucy slow down and play less strenuous games for Peyton's sake. Lucy was unhappy, and it caused us stress." She shifted to the edge of the chair, her courage rising. "And do you remember how upset you were when I told Peyton about her body and what was about to happen?"

"But I apologized for that, Kelsey. I was being stupid."

"I know you said you were sorry, but that's the problem. We get along great. We have a wonderful relationship, but I don't think it will work, Ross. We'll spend our lives resenting our motivation and behavior, trying to please each other and both girls. It's an impossible situation."

"Impossible? We've been doing it for months." He pushed himself up from the sofa and crossed to her side. "Kelsey, it works. We don't have to cater to the girls. They're doing well now. Peyton's out of my bedroom and in her own—"

"It has nothing to do with the bedroom." Her stomach churned and nausea caught in her throat.

"Yes, it does. I coddled Peyton. Remember? But I've changed, and I'm happy I did. Peyton's happier. She feels more normal, and she's doing well. Lucy is, too. The girls are friends now. They're like sisters, and Peyton told me you're like a mother to her." He knelt at her feet. "Do you hear what I'm saying?"

Tears churned in her eyes and clung to her lashes. "Yes, but—"

He grasped her hands. "I haven't complained, have I?" He searched her face.

"No."

"We've talked about this before. Two are better than one. If one falls, the friend can help the other one up." He lifted her hand and kissed her fingers. "Kelsey, we are a three-strand cord as the Bible says. It's you, me and God. We're not alone with our struggles, and look how blessed we are."

His voice quaked, and Kelsey couldn't hold back the tears. All the thoughts, the fears she'd had for the past weeks seemed so empty and weak when she viewed Ross's strength. He understood God's ways so much better than she did.

He touched her cheek. "Yes, we may have to deal with more illness—I pray we don't—but we have the Lord and each other. We're not easily broken."

She felt broken. Every ounce of strength she'd garnered failed her. Her decisiveness failed as she looked in Ross's eyes. "But I'm broken, Ross. I can't let go of that fear. Doug walked out on me, and I thought we had a solid marriage. He abandoned us." She searched his eyes. "I trust you, Ross, but I..."

"You're afraid. Worried." He drew her closer. "God is my witness, Kelsey. I love you and Lucy with all my heart. I would never hurt you." He kissed the end of her nose. "You're being the practical Kelsey I first met. I watched you struggle to look at life with your heart, but you've had a setback. Instead of your heart, you're trying to reason everything out. Some things can't be reasoned. They're felt."

Head and heart. She had struggled. Kelsey gazed into his eyes, realizing he knew her better than she knew herself. "But I don't want you to be miserable with my idiosyncrasies."

"I've grown to love them." He tightened his embrace. "I think of them fondly as your idiot-syncrasies."

The sweet sound of his voice lifted her spirit. "Thanks."

"You're welcome." He tilted her chin upward. "The Lord doesn't promise we'll have sunshine every day, but He promises that He's with us every day—rain or shine."

A ragged breath escaped her. "I know."

"He also gave us a sense of humor. You put up with me and my idiot-syncrasies, too. We all have them, you know. But yours are part of you, and I love them."

He loved them. The words washed over her. She'd never met a person who loved even her quirks, but Ross did. "I'm confused and so sorry. I feel lost without you, and I think that scares me. What happens if you can't handle me after a while and decide to—?"

He pressed his index finger on her lips. "I will never walk out on you, Kelsey. Neither you nor Lucy. When I make a commitment, it's from the heart, and that's what counts." Ross slipped his finger from her mouth and replaced it with his lips.

From the heart, and that's what counts. She melted against his frame, yielding to his kiss. In his arms she felt complete. That was another thing that couldn't be reasoned.

"See you next week." Kelsey stood near the door, glad that her year as moderator had come to a close. Voting in a new leader and a new name—Parents of Special Kids—had been her final task.

Ross slipped past her with one of the other fathers, a newer one he'd taken under his wing. "Meet you outside."

She adored his compassionate way of listening and now his ability to share his real feelings. So many men had found their way to the meeting and were learning to reveal their emotions.

"Thanks for all your hard work."

She turned from the hallway. "Thanks, Ava." Ava had run

for moderator, but had been outvoted. One of the newer ladies was now the moderator. "I hope you're okay with the vote."

"The vote. I'm thrilled. After I agreed to run, I knew I'd made a mistake."

"Really." Kelsey found that hard to believe. Ava had always been their question lady. Nothing slipped past her without a multitude of questions that dug so deep into the topic that everyone longed to go home. But she'd been faithful to the group and a likeable woman otherwise.

"I don't want to be in charge. I'd prefer to look at things from a different viewpoint and dig into it. I'd have to be unbiased as moderator. That's hard for me to do."

Amazed at her self-awareness, Kelsey gave her a hug. "Questions have always been your forte. We all know that."

She chuckled. "Although I drive you all crazy sometimes." She shook her finger. "Don't think I don't know."

Her smile assured Kelsey that she had no hard feelings. "See you next week."

She gave a wave and left.

Kelsey drew in a deep breath, relaxed her shoulders and turned off the light. The summer sun had reappeared from behind the morning clouds, and she longed to be outside. Home was more like it. They'd left the two girls at her house alone.

Ross gave her a wave when she stepped outside. He shook hands with the other father and strode her way. "Don't tell me. You're worried about the girls."

She chuckled. "Not worried exactly. Just anxious to get home."

Since they'd met, Ross could somehow read her mind. Maybe it was her face. But he seemed to know what she was thinking. She wasn't sure if that was good or bad.

He opened the car door for her and she slipped in. Their talk had grown easy in the past month, since she'd shaken the fear that had paralyzed her. Ross's words often filled her mind. A cord of three strands is not easily broken. Both girls were doing great. Lucy had healed well from her surgery, and her hair had already begun to grow back. It was all more than she could have wished for, and she rejoiced with Ross that Peyton had made great strides, as well.

"I should never have listened to people's fears about us." She gazed into his beguiling eyes. "And my own irrational fears."

"Huh?" He gave her a questioning look. "Where did that come from today?"

"I was thinking how well the girls are doing now. And they're friends. Better friends than we had ever hoped." He smiled, and her heart soared.

Ross squeezed her hand. "I'm going to drop you off at the house and then run a quick errand."

"Errand? I'm going to make lunch. Aren't you going to eat?"

"I'll be back in a few minutes. I know you're anxious to get home."

She eyed him, her curiosity piqued. "Don't do that. I can spare a—"

He swung down her street. "No, it's fine. I'll drop you off."

She slipped from the minivan, wishing she had the knack he did for mind reading. Something was fishy. She waited as he drove down the street, stymied as to what his secret mission was all about.

The house sounded empty. "Lucy?"

Nothing.

She dropped her purse on the sofa and strode into the kitchen. No mess. That was odd. She snapped her fingers, walked to the breakfast nook and pushed back the curtains. She relaxed. The girls were sitting on the new glider Ross had bought for the backyard after Lucy complained that she had nowhere to sit and read. Kelsey wondered what was wrong with a lawn chair, but Ross coddled her. *Coddled.* She shook her head and chuckled.

Lunch consisted of tuna and egg salad, bread, lettuce and homemade cookies for dessert. She didn't plan to fuss. As she pulled the items from the refrigerator and grabbed plates from the cabinet, she heard Ross come through the door. He slipped to her side, drawing her into his arms.

Before she could speak, his lips met hers, and she indulged in his amazing kiss. His arms held her close, his mouth moved on hers as soft as a summer breeze.

He eased back and grinned. "How would you like to be greeted like that every day?"

"By you?"

He ruffled her hair. "Who else?"

She chuckled. "I'd love it."

"Good."

She paused, trying to dig into his thoughts, but failed. "Call the girls." He stepped toward the bedrooms. "They're in the back, languishing on the glider."

He grinned and did what she asked.

The clomping footsteps told her the girls had come inside.

"Mom, this is the best book." Lucy waved her novel in the air. "It's about this girl who wins a contest and gets to have her dream-come-true vacation."

"I'll go for that." Peyton waved her hand in the air. "When do we leave?"

"Not for a while yet," Ross said.

All eyes turned to him. Kelsey's heart felt ready to burst. "What does that mean?"

"Sit." He waved to the island where she'd set out the food. "I want to show you something." He walked into the living room.

The girls each jumped up on a stool, and Kelsey passed around the plates. As the girls began to build their sandwiches, Ross came in carrying a white box and set it on the breakfast table.

Kelsey craned her neck. "What's that?"

"That's second. This is first." He dug into his pocket and pulled out a smaller box.

Her heart skipped, and she pressed her hand to her chest. "Don't tell me…"

"I won't have to if you open it." He handed it to her.

The girls lost interest in their sandwiches. They both slid off the stools and drew closer, their eyes shifting from Ross to the box.

"Open it, Mom."

Kelsey's fingers shook as she lifted the lid, knowing what she would see. She held her breath and gazed inside at the small, velvet, blue ring box.

"What is it?" Peyton shifted to look over her shoulder. "I think it's jewelry."

Lucy clapped her hands. "It's a ring, isn't it?"

Kelsey grinned at Ross, his face beaming.

He arched his brows. "She'd know if she'd open the lid."

She did and gazed at the magnificent diamond, the gold band adorned with diamond baguettes. "Ross, it's beautiful."

The girls' eyes were as large as the saucers beneath their sandwiches. "It's an engagement ring." Their voices blended as one.

Ross applauded. "You're right." He moved closer to Kelsey and removed the ring from the velvet. "You're pretty high up on that stool, but here goes." He knelt on the kitchen tile, his gaze locked with hers. "Kelsey Rhodes, would you do me the honor of becoming Mrs. Ross Salburg?"

She slipped from the stool and knelt beside him. "Absolutely."

Their lips met as the girls squealed and jumped around them. Peyton's voice cut through Lucy's cheers. "Now we're really sisters."

Lucy's squeal subsided. "We are."

They threw their arms around each other and spun around the room until Kelsey had to call their antics to a halt. "You'll break your necks."

"Anyway, I have something else for all of us." Ross walked to the breakfast table and returned with the box.

The girls dropped their embrace, their gazes flitting from Kelsey to Ross.

Kelsey eyed the logo on the cover from a florist shop. While Ross lifted the lid, she and the girls waited. Her heart swelled with happiness.

Ross reached in and pulled out a Hawaiian lei and draped it over her neck. Then he slipped one over Lucy's head and another over Peyton's. They eyed the lovely circle of baby orchids and stared at him. "Dreams Come True has offered to give our daughters a special trip to—"

"Hawaii." Peyton's and Lucy's voices split the air.

"Dad, really?" Peyton tugged on his arm.

Lucy stood looking at him, her mouth gaping. "But what about Mom?"

Ross gazed at Kelsey and closed the distance between them. He slipped his arms around her. "She has to be there. It's her honeymoon."

Her mind spun. A honeymoon in Hawaii—and with the girls. "You couldn't have planned anything better."

He held up his hand. "But I refused the offer."

The room silenced.

"I thought the money could go to a child whose parents can't afford a trip."

"Really?" Peyton's sad eyes gazed at him.

Kelsey leaned toward him, her mind snapping. "You really did this?"

He nodded.

"Did you talk with the donor? Do you know who he is?"

"No, I spoke with Ethan. He understands. And why would I know the donor?"

"You're friends with Ethan. Maybe he knows and just won't say."

Ross shook his head. "No one does as far as I know."

Kelsey acknowledged that he was telling the truth. The elusive donor. Would anyone ever know?

"Dad, then we're not going?" Peyton's plaintive voice tugged at Kelsey's heart.

He chuckled. "Sure we are." He bent and kissed Kelsey's hair. "All we need to do is set the date."

"Now."

"Soon."

Kelsey gazed into his eyes. "Very soon."

The girls ran to them, the four of them surged into one giant embrace and Kelsey reveled in the gift. God, as always, guided their paths. She'd learned the hard way. And she knew that two were much, much better than one. Four, even better.

"I love you, Kelsey." His whisper feathered her ear.

She brushed his lips with hers. "I love you, too, and I promise this from my heart."

* * * * *

Dear Reader,

This series has been a challenge to bring you a story that you can enjoy with a happy ending and yet tell the story of parents dealing with seriously ill children. But this is life for many people who face each day with hope and fear. I decided to challenge both Kelsey and Ross with a romance that added another challenge—two children with debilitating diseases. I researched these serious illnesses and hope I have presented them accurately. If not, I apologize. Life often brings problems to each of us—illnesses, death and losses of all kinds in our distressed economy—but we have one constant assurance. We are never alone. The Lord is by our side with love and mercy, carrying our burdens when we ask and offering us life eternal. No matter how difficult our troubles are on earth, we have God at our side. We are forever blessed.

Gail Gaymer Martin

Questions for Discussion

1. Kelsey and Ross met for the first time and felt an immediate connection. Have you ever met someone and liked that person right away? How can this happen?

2. Kelsey and Ross seemed destined for each other. He'd shown an interest in MOSK, he knew Ethan and he was the best man at Ethan's wedding. They questioned if this was God's doing. If it was, why would the Lord guide two people together like this?

3. What strengths do Kelsey and Ross have that support each other?

4. "Two are better than one" from Ecclesiastes 4:9 is a theme in this novel. Have you found this to be a truth in your life? If so, in what ways?

5. If a person has never married, how does "Two is better than one" still fit into the person's life?

6. Have you or someone you know had to face life with a severely ill child? What keeps people going in this situation? What gives them strength?

7. Ross struggled with Peyton's new medication. It offered him both pros and cons. Kelsey sometimes felt the same way about her situation with Lucy. What fears did they struggle with?

8. Have you experienced a situation in your life when learning the truth frightened you as much as not knowing? What kind of circumstances would arouse these fears?

9. Kelsey felt gullible and stupid, not realizing that her husband was cheating on her. How can someone miss the clues? Have you missed clues in your relationships?

10. Peyton and Lucy were typical preteens. What characteristics did you see in them to prove this?

11. Peyton was a lonely girl in the beginning of the novel. When you were young, did you ever feel the way she did in school or when it came to making friends?

12. Were you surprised when Ross decided not to take the Dreams Come True trip, but pay for it himself? Why would he do this?

13. Ava Darnell, a member of MOSK and a secondary character in this novel, will be the heroine in the next book of the Dreams Come True series. What do you know about Ava that could make her an interesting character?

14. Have you found any plot threads in this series that have yet to be answered? What are they? Do you think you might learn the answer in the final novel in the series?

INSPIRATIONAL

Inspirational romances to warm your heart & soul.

TITLES AVAILABLE NEXT MONTH

Available September 27, 2011

REQUEST YOUR FREE BOOKS!

2 FREE INSPIRATIONAL NOVELS
PLUS 2
FREE
MYSTERY GIFTS

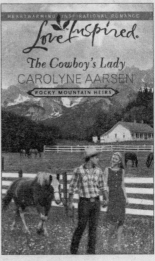